The Secret of Delta Pavonis

By: Joshua McCullough

Nonpareil Institute
Practical Autism Solutions

The Secret of Delta Pavonis

Author: Joshua McCullough
Editor: Christopher J. Murray
Artist: Lyndon Willoughby

Nonpareil Institute
5240 Tennyson Parkway, Suite 105
Plano, TX 75024
www.npitx.org

ISBN: 978-0-9884184-9-3

To my late grandmother,
the first to read this book.

Table of Contents

PROLOGUE

The massive ship floated serenely in the void of space, gently circling the green and blue world below. The time had finally come. Humanity had outgrown its cradle, and overcrowding now necessitated that they set out across the sea of stars to seek new worlds to inhabit. Great colony ships had been commissioned and constructed to this end, and *Spirit of Hope* was one such ship.

Its destination was relatively close to Earth in astronomical terms, only twenty light years away. Using conventional propulsion, it would be far out of reach, but the creation of the subspace immersion engine, or SIE, had changed all that. It would now take the great vessel only fifteen years to reach its destination: Pavonis Prime. During that time, the crew and passengers would rest in the cold embrace of cryogenic capsules.

The ship would be tended to throughout its journey by its complement of artificially intelligent robots. These robots were another recent technological breakthrough, and their presence would be invaluable as the colonists worked to tame their new home. The ship's complement of plants and animals, carefully selected from Earth's diverse biosphere and placed in stasis like the passengers, would also be essential to the success of their efforts.

Their destination was a planet remarkably like their own. It was a water-bearing world, slightly further from its sun than Earth was from its own. It had three small moons orbiting it. There were few candidate planets so close to Earth that matched human needs so well. These colonists were fortunate to have been selected for this particular world.

The final few shuttles bearing passengers and supplies to the massive vessel were docking now, ready to deliver their loads and allow the great ship to depart. As soon as they finished, the journey would begin. Sealed in the icy shells of their pods, the colonists dreamed of better futures and wide open expanses.

Spirit of Hope finally lumbered into motion, its mechanical frame groaning in protest as it maneuvered out of Earth's gravity well, and into position to engage its SIE drive. The ponderous leviathan seemed to stretch as the drive engaged, before vanishing in a blink, committed to its flight into the unknown.

Chapter 1

"Hey, Alex, watch your six!" George's voice squawked through the headset in Alex Morris' ear. Alex glanced at his scopes and cursed the moment of inattentiveness that had let the enemy ship slip in behind him. Alex did his best to shake his pursuer, but it stubbornly remained directly aft. Two more slivers of angry light sizzled past, mere centimeters above his wing.

"I can't shake him off. Mind taking care of him?" Alex asked his wingman, George Simmons, who had alerted him to the enemy ship in the first place.

"Sure thing, but you owe me one," George replied, pulling in behind Alex's pursuer and pumping brilliant bolts of ruby light into its hull until it expanded in a silent explosion.

"Another wave inbound. All craft move to intercept," their flight instructor announced. "I don't want any of them getting through." Tension filled his voice, and with good reason. They had already fought through two waves of enemies, and the battle was taking its toll on both man and machine. Several defending ships showed heavy damage, with pilots struggling to retain control over their crippled craft.

"You heard him," Victoria, Alex's squadron leader, called out. "Move to engage." Her calm, clear tone steadied the frayed nerves of the pilots and fortified their confidence. Alex and his squad mates trusted in her ability to see them through this engagement.

Alex spun his fighter around toward the new contacts, the cold blackness of space swirling around him. He loved the responsiveness of this new fighter model. It handled better and hit harder than the relics he and the other cadets had been stuck with before. This *Valkyrie*-class was an upgrade he could get used to. Its sleek, curved, crescent-like wings gleamed white against the void, while its blunt, dark-blue nose stretched out in front of him. This ship lived up to its name in every way, like a deadly avatar of battle—a chosen warrior of the gods.

The craft shook from an impact and Alex checked his instruments, confused. He was still too far out to take a hit, wasn't he? He turned his eyes back to the main screen, only to see more shots incoming from the target vessels looming still so far ahead of them. Like a sudden downpour, a deadly rain of energy cascaded around them.

"Evasive action!" Victoria shouted over the com, as several of the *Valkyries* around Alex vanished in expanding balls of fire.

"What the hell is going on?" George cried out.

"We're dead," Liz moaned. A chaotic chorus of panicked voices erupted over the com. All protocol forgotten, each of the carefully organized squadrons lapsed into complete anarchy.

"Cut the chatter and approach at maximum burn! Engage as soon as you come into range!" Victoria cut them off, angrily. The channel went silent, but the damage was done. Six more ships had met their end, and many of the remaining fighters were out of formation. Their recently fortified morale was now shot.

Any semblance of a battle was gone. This was a straight-up slaughter. Off his wing, Alex saw George's fighter take a bolt straight through the cockpit. The craft veered slowly away, still functional, but without a pilot to direct it. Another ship, riddled with holes, vanished in a torrent of murderous energy. Stifling a curse, Alex focused his attention forward once more. Distractions would only lead to his own elimination, so he focused all his concentration on navigating through the deadly storm. He felt a strange sensation in his head, like an awareness he had never achieved before.

Webs of angry, red light lanced past Alex as he fought to close the distance to his target: the large dropship full of hostile robots intent on taking away his only home, the moon called Ymir. He could feel his heart pounding in his chest, and found that it was hard to breathe. The distance to his target fell away agonizingly slowly, seconds feeling like hours. He evaded the incoming fire as if standing outside in a hurricane, trying to dodge the innumerable raindrops. A shot caught his left wing and wrenched his ship sideways as the wing came apart in chunks. The cockpit illuminated blindingly bright as another bolt caught his ship dead center.

# # #

Alex sat in the darkness of his sealed flight simulator, a fine, cold sweat covering his skin. He felt exhausted, as if he had just swum across an ocean. He pulled off his now-muggy helmet, and replayed the engagement in his head. If that was all he and his fellow classmates at the academy had to show for themselves, then they clearly had a long way to go before they would be piloting real fighters. Some of the others were probably complaining right now about the simulation "cheating," but Alex felt he understood the point the academy's instructors had intended to make:

This wasn't just a game. Real lives would be at stake after they graduated. Growing complacent and being unable to react to the unexpected would endanger the entire Ymir colony. After the original colony's robots had gone berserk fifty years ago and driven everyone off Pavonis Prime, humanity had been clinging to life on the planet's three moons, weathering constant assaults from the crazed machines below.

Despite this reality, Alex couldn't help feeling slightly upset that the instructors had chosen this moment to drive the point home. His class had been doing so well up until now! The cockpit canopy slowly began to lift, allowing the overhead illumination of the drab training facility to spill in from its high ceiling. He pulled himself out of the simulator pod with a bit of stiffness and made his way down the bright, yellow ladder attached to the side.

He saw Victoria headed his way with a sour expression, and prepared himself for the inevitable. He wasn't at all in the mood for one of her verbal lashings, but there was really no way around it. Victoria was tall—taller than him, at least, which irked him—with long, blonde hair and pale blue eyes that seemed to pierce right through him. Her dark-blue flight suit was still immaculate somehow, unlike his sweat-drenched one.

"I've told you all a hundred times not to get complacent, haven't I?" she began. "I knew they'd throw us a curveball sooner or later. Anyway, come on. They're waiting on us to debrief."

"That's it?" Alex blurted out, and then mentally kicked himself for it. If she was going to go easy on him this time, who was he to stop her? Although, he had to admit, many times her dreaded lectures were entirely warranted.

"What's that supposed to mean?" Victoria asked, looking almost as if Alex had slapped her. It was extremely uncharacteristic of Victoria, who never let anyone get under her skin.

"You were the last one shot down," she continued, no longer displaying any trace of emotion, "I can't really be upset with you if you managed to last longer than I did, *this time*." She placed extra emphasis on the last two words, as if to assure both of them that this was an exception to the norm. "Come on, let's go."

Even if it was a fluke, being the last pilot shot down took some of the sting out of the massacre they had just gone through. They made their way through the halls of the academy in silence, walking side by side. Alex found himself wondering why Victoria had even waited for him at all.

The other cadets were indeed already there as Alex and Victoria walked into the classroom where debriefings were held after simulator exercises. Alex quietly slipped into a seat near the back of the room, and Victoria, who usually sat up front, took the desk next to him. Alex thought he understood why after that debacle. Like the rest of the class, he and Victoria waited in silence for the debriefing session to begin. The other cadets sat at their desks showing varying degrees of concern (or lack thereof), from George's bored, relaxed expression to Liz's pale face as she squirmed in her seat. At the front of the room, Commander Prescott stood impatiently, a dissatisfied scowl engraved on his narrow face. His sharp, hawkish nose and piercing grey eyes made him all the more intimidating to the cadets, and they were matched by his strict, severe personality. His gaze swept across the room like a spotlight, those caught in it invariably flinching or turning away. Except Victoria, of course.

Wonderful, Alex thought morosely, *if Prescott is running this session, it'll be more of an inquisition than a debriefing.*

"Let's begin," Commander Prescott started the session off abruptly. "I am constantly surprised by the poor performance of this class, and I would think I would have grown used to it by now, but your incompetence is seemingly without bounds." Several cadets winced at the stinging rebuke. This was their first year at the academy, which followed mandatorily after the requisite education from six to fifteen years of age. With such a small population, everyone, with very few exceptions, was expected to serve in the armed forces for a minimum of two years.

"Miss Barrett," Prescott continued, addressing Victoria directly, "you were placed in command of this operation. Perhaps you can enlighten me as to the reason behind your spectacular failure." He crossed his arms and held her in the grip of his narrowed eyes.

Victoria stood, her emotions hidden behind an expressionless face. If she felt at all intimidated by the instructor, she gave no sign. Victoria always seemed cool and collected under pressure.

"Sir," she began, "the operation proceeded smoothly and by the book, up until the last wave of enemy ships which displayed capabilities not previously encountered. My squadron was caught off-guard and killed in the resulting confusion." It was a politician's answer, Alex thought. Victoria's father, Councilman Marcus Barrett, was one of the most prominent leaders of the Ymir Council. Victoria's explanation for their defeat was worthy of him for sure.

As for the simulation, the instructors occasionally threw them a curveball by altering the program in some way, but this had been rather extreme. There really wasn't much more Victoria could have done. The cadets were simply too green to handle a non-textbook scenario like the one they had just been given.

"Being able to handle such situations is vital to survival on the battlefield, for a soldier, and especially for a commander," Prescott rebutted, sweeping the room with his eyes as he spoke, and turning his piercing gaze on Victoria to punctuate the last part. He turned his attention to another cadet.

"Mr. Collins, your performance was by far the worst in this exercise. The other cadets at least made it to the final portion of the exam. You, however, were killed in action exactly..." he checked the report on the terminal before him, "forty-seven seconds into the engagement. Can you explain yourself?"

"No sir." The extremely nervous cadet couldn't even raise his head to meet the instructor's eyes. He squirmed in his seat as if the look of disapproval in Prescott's eyes physically pained him. Several awkward seconds passed as the instructor let his gaze skewer the boy unmercifully before he finally relented.

"I thought as much," Commander Prescott replied. "Lastly," he consulted the report once more. "Mr. Morris," he turned to Alex, a note of mock surprise in his voice, "you managed to outlast the rest of the class by over two minutes. It seems miracles do occasionally happen."

Alex blinked. Had it really been that long?

Prescott again addressed the entire room. "Your failure in this exercise highlights the deficiencies of this class, and therefore we will be holding remedial sessions to bring you all up to speed," He glared around the room as if daring anyone to protest. "Very well then, dismissed." He turned and walked stiffly out of the classroom.

As soon as he left, the tension in the room burst like a bubble, and a dull roar of conversation broke out. Alex looked up as George approached his desk. His friend and roommate was taller even than Victoria, and quite lanky. He had dark skin, and curly black hair atop his head. The sleeves and legs of his flight suit exposed a fair bit of his forearms and ankles. *He must have grown again,* Alex noted. George's suit itself was somewhat disheveled. Laundry was a sporadic thing for George. For some reason he had a big grin on his face.

"Let's get some lunch," George said, "on you, of course."

"Oh, and why is that?" Alex asked.

"I told you in the sim," George replied, smiling even wider, "you owe me one, and I'm collecting." Clearly, the matter was non-negotiable.

"Fine," Alex groaned, "whatever." He supposed George had earned this much. Without his timely assist during the simulation, Alex likely would not have survived half as long as he had.

Victoria stood up and moved purposefully over to Alex's desk, "Honestly, George, if you spent half as much time in the sims as you do thinking about your stomach you'd be the top of the class by now." George consistently placed in the top ten spots on the board, so reaching the top spot was actually within the realm of possibility for him, Alex supposed. *Unlike my own prospects,* he reminded himself with just a touch of bitterness.

"Not likely," George snorted, "if you thought your spot on top of the board was in jeopardy you'd double your own sim time to stay ahead." Victoria had pretty much claimed the top spot in the class since the very beginning, which was the primary reason she had been in charge of this, and most other simulator missions. Her superiority was just a fact of life now, and the other cadets had pretty much given up on trying to usurp her.

"Let's go, then," Alex offered, not wanting to get caught in the midst of a battle of egos between George and Victoria. He stood up and started heading for the door. George and Victoria fell in behind him.

"Paul, Liz, Claire, you coming?" Alex called out to their other friends. Paul and Liz stood a short distance away, standing on either side of Claire's desk.

"Sure, why not." Paul replied easily, sweeping his mess of brown hair out of his pale green eyes. Claire smiled brightly. The three of them joined the group as they headed out. Liz looked especially glad to be leaving the debriefing room. She was the shortest of the group, with straight, mousy, brown hair, which she always left down, and green eyes. She was very timid and introverted. She had essentially joined the circle of friends by association through Claire, with whom she had always been close. Claire was, in fact, walking next to her now. With an athletic build and average height, Claire was not unattractive. Her wavy blonde hair extended to just above her shoulders and her blue eyes were friendly and inviting.

They made their way out of the academy facility and across the grounds of the military ward. The ward housed all military facilities, from the fighter hangars to the barracks, to the academy where Alex and the others were currently training for their compulsory service. Nearly a quarter of the colony's population served in the operation of the military base in some way at any given time. From fighter pilots, to cooks and secretaries, everyone was expected to do their part to ensure the Ymir colony's survival.

Just as Alex turned toward the mess hall, Victoria exclaimed, "I don't think I can tolerate that swill today. Let's head into town."

"Easy for you to say," Claire returned, "you can afford to be picky." She had a point. Most of the cadets were limited by the meager allowance they earned while training, but since Victoria's father was as wealthy as he was adept at politics, she never had to worry about money.

"I'll cover you, then," Victoria offered, glancing at Alex. "If that's the problem don't worry about it."

Alex kept walking toward the mess hall. "I don't feel like heading into town," he said, "I'll see you all later," he glanced back to see George still walking alongside him, and the others staring at them perplexedly. For a moment, he could have sworn Victoria looked hurt by his decision, but her expression returned to its usual unreadable mask quickly, so he shrugged it off.

"Alright," she called, "suit yourself." The group turned and started out toward the city.

"What are you tagging along for?" Alex queried George. "You too good for Victoria's money?" His friend had kept pace with him as he broke off from the group and was walking alongside him.

"Yeah, right," George shot back, making a face. "I bet you forgot you still owe me a lunch, and I aim to collect on that." He clapped a hand on Alex's shoulder as he spoke, to punctuate the statement.

Alex sighed. "Let's get this over with." He could see the mess hall ahead, a drab, squat, grey building, unimpressive amongst the other military facilities. The Ymir colony's flag hung listlessly on the pole in front of the building. It consisted of a white background, with a dark blue circle centered on it. A lighter blue equilateral triangle stood within the circle. Alex found himself wondering, yet again, what the point was of raising the flag beneath the colony's protective dome where no wind would ever rouse it.

It was noon, and military personnel of every rank and station packed the mess hall, sitting around tables and enjoying the short break from their daily routines. As they waited in line, George bemoaned their fate. "Remedial lessons? Ridiculous! That was a really lame move they pulled on us. We were doing so well. They just had to kick us in the teeth."

"Don't take it personally," Alex replied. "I'm pretty sure Prescott designed that sim, and he hates everyone." Alex knew it wasn't the extra workload bothering his friend. The implication behind "remedial lessons" had bruised George's ego.

"Well I'll be real glad once we've graduated and I never have to see his face again." George scowled, likely picturing the instructor's gaunt visage in his head. "The sooner we're out, the happier I'll be."

"No argument there," Alex said in agreement. He paid for both their meals as they reached the end of the line, and then hefted his tray. "Come on, let's find a table."

# # #

Paul, Liz, and Claire had followed along as Victoria made her way off-base to downtown Nifelheim, humanity's small sanctuary on this bleak ball of ice called Ymir. Even after fifty years, the city maintained a stark, utilitarian appearance. Resources were scarce on Ymir, so structures were built without any expense spared for aesthetics. Excepting, of course, she mused, the section dedicated to the upper crust like her father. The lavish homes of the politicians who governed the colony stood in stark contrast to their Spartan surroundings. Then, her thoughts turned to Alex and his refusal of her invitation.

"Did you have a place in mind?" Claire asked, interrupting Victoria's musings.

"There's a place over in fourth district which is fairly nice," Victoria replied after a moment of reflection. "Let's head there." Her companions seemed to be a few shades paler than they had been a moment before.

"Aren't we a bit underdressed for that kind of place?" Liz asked, worriedly.

"Don't worry about it," Victoria assured her friend. "We're friends of the owner." It was at least somewhat true. At least, everyone she had met wanted to be considered a friend of her father's. Although they only seemed half convinced by her assurances, her friends voiced no further concerns, and so they continued on quietly.

"Isn't that..." Liz voiced, pointing toward a group headed the opposite direction across the street from them.

Victoria looked to where Liz was pointing. "Yes, it looks like it," she confirmed. Honestly, it was just as uncommon a sight for her as it was for the others. Sandwiched between a pair of armed soldiers walked a girl who appeared to be around their age of sixteen, though Victoria couldn't quite tell due to the large, silver helmet covering the girl's head, as well as her eyes and nose. Several wires ran from the back of it, connecting to various points on her spine and arms. Seeing one of the psychics, referred to as "gifted," being escorted in broad daylight was very unusual.

Victoria recalled what little the academy had told them about gifted. Apparently, they were a new phenomenon, only appearing since the first colony had been established on Pavonis Prime. There had been no confirmed cases of these psychics on Earth prior to their departure. No one knew exactly what it was about the Delta Pavonis system that had caused them to suddenly show up. The air? The water? Something else entirely?

The psionic research center, headquartered here in Nifelheim, had been established to answer those questions. Infants here and in the colonies on the other two moons, Eden and Adar, were tested, and if they possessed psionic abilities, they were brought here to the center for research. Gifted had played a large role in fending off the original AI attacks on Pavonis Prime long enough for the colonists to evacuate. All of the colonies agreed that cultivation of these abilities for military application was in everyone's best interests. Except, of course, some of the families as their children were taken away, but they really needed to look at the big picture, or so Victoria thought.

Victoria stood and watched the soldiers escort the girl past them. As they passed, the girl abruptly turned her head directly toward Victoria. With the helmet on, the girl couldn't really lock eyes with her, but that was exactly how it felt. The girl's gaze seemed to bore straight through the helmet and on through Victoria as well. It felt like minutes, but only a moment had passed, before the girl turned away again and proceeded on wordlessly.

"Creepy," Claire breathed a moment later, "what was that about?"

"Who knows?" Victoria focused on speaking clearly and calmly although she felt a bit shaken. No need to let anyone else see her shook up. "Come on, let's go."

# # #

A girl sat rigidly in a cold, metal chair, the sole piece of furniture in an examination room in the Psionic Research Center. She waited patiently for the next test to begin, seemingly not bothered by the various sensors and electrodes placed on her skin, nor by the heavy-looking metal helmet covering her head, blocking her vision completely. The only name given to her was Subject 148, and she had spent her entire life in this building. She turned her head to glance toward the window the researchers stood behind. Though her eyes were covered, she had other ways of seeing. There were four this time, going over the data from the most recent test. One of them turned toward her and pressed a button on his console, opening the door to the test chamber. "That will be all for now, 148," he said. "Return to your quarters." Wordlessly, 148 peeled the electrodes from her skin and stood, allowing the guards to escort her away.

They moved down the sterile, white corridor silently. The guards never spoke to her, and she had never had any reason to speak to them. They were completely unnecessary, as she knew the way back to her room very well, but she had never protested their presence. She saw no reason to do so. They stepped into the elevator at the end of the hall, and one of the guards ran his security card through the scanner, selecting a floor. The elevator hummed quietly as they dropped deeper into the complex. After a short while, the doors opened again and they stepped out into a nearly identical hallway. They moved on through a series of turns, which would likely confuse anyone who had not spent a great deal of time here. All of the corridors appeared the same. Only the numbers alongside the doors changed. Finally, they stepped into the "residential" section of the complex reserved for the test subjects. They reached the door with her number, one hundred forty-eight, and the door slid aside as the guard, once again, scanned his security pass. Subject 148 stepped inside and the door slid quietly shut behind her, locked from the outside. She sat lightly on the edge of her bed, and then lay back on it. The doctors always advised that she take every opportunity to rest between tests, and she did so, dropping into sleep now with little effort.

# # #

Victoria returned home to her father's mansion later that afternoon to find her father waiting for her. He was seated in their luxurious living room situated near the front door, in which they typically received guests.

"Victoria," he began, a frown creasing his face, "when I allowed you to enroll in the academy, it was with the impression that you would make a good showing and do our family proud." He held up a display he had been reading from. "These latest results are not very encouraging."

"I have maintained my place at the top of the rankings, father," Victoria replied. "Everyone was marked poorly on this exam." It was the truth, after all. She remembered George's ribbing about her scores earlier. Little did he and the others know that placing so highly was the only reason she was able to remain in the academy at all. Unlike most of the cadets, her attendance there was entirely her decision, and now that choice was, once again, being threatened by her father.

"I understand that, of course, "he continued, "However they were not placed in command of the operation." He sighed. "You must understand, it will reflect poorly on us—" *by which he means himself,* Victoria mentally interjected. "—if the public sees a Barrett fail in a leadership position."

"I understand that father," she said, "and I assure you that it won't happen again. Surely you can explain away one mistake!" She spoke imploringly. She needed him to understand, but that was too much to hope for, so at least she needed him to accept this and to give her another chance.

He considered her plea for a moment, rubbing his chin thoughtfully. "Very well," he relented, "see that it doesn't happen again. Now go and get yourself ready for the dinner I'm hosting tonight." He turned back the reader display in his hands. Clearly he was done with her for the moment.

Well, she told herself, *time to throw on my public face and rub elbows with the other members of the upper class. No problem,* she assured herself as she headed out of the room. *No problem.*

# # #

Victoria paused for a moment before entering the large ballroom, making one last check to ensure she looked presentable. She was grateful that she could now wear her military dress uniform to social functions instead of those elaborate and uncomfortable dresses. Her father even encouraged this, highlighting the family's dedication to the military, throwing it in the faces of some present who had exempted their children from service. Everything was political to him. Everything. That wasn't to say Victoria disapproved. No, she was certainly her father's daughter, and she drew the same thrill from this elaborate game. Drawing a deep breath, she forced a warm smile onto her face and entered the fray.

"Ah, Victoria, there you are!" her father, Marcus Barrett, beckoned her over. His once dark hair was now streaked with grey, which gave him a distinguished look, and matched the steel grey of his eyes. Victoria had inherited her height from her father, though not its full extent; he towered over even her. Her hair and eyes, on the other hand, were her late mother's. "This is Ambassador Gerard Harris of Eden colony. Ambassador, Victoria, my daughter."

"A pleasure," the ambassador smiled, taking her proffered hand. "I recognize you from the science fair, of course!" Victoria smiled. The science fair was held yearly and children of all ages from all three colonies competed if they were in school. Victoria had won every time. People on all three colonies knew who she was, and recognized her genius.

The ambassador's appearance was typical for a resident of the Eden colony, in stark contrast to the residents of Ymir.

Like most from the lush, jungle world, he spent far more time outdoors, as evidenced by his tanned skin. His smooth hands, however, assured her that time was primarily for leisure, and certainly not for toiling in the vast agricultural fields that produced most of the food for the three colonies.

"Ah," her father exclaimed, "there's the duke of Adar. Excuse me." He headed away through the crowd to attend to his other guests. Left to entertain the ambassador on her own, Victoria endeavored to engage him in small talk.

"I have heard so much about the tropical climate on Eden," she began, "I hope the dreariness of Nifelheim is not too unpleasant for you, ambassador."

Ambassador Harris smiled in response. "I do find myself missing the fresh air at times," he confessed to her, "but a visit to your impressive greenhouses or a walk around the Eden Embassy helps to alleviate that somewhat. I confess, though, that I do not relish the thought of setting foot outside. I don't have much tolerance for the cold."

"I'm sure there is little opportunity to develop that tolerance on Eden," Victoria replied with an easy laugh. "How does our fair city compare, I wonder? Favorably, I would hope."

"It is a marvel of technology," the ambassador admitted. "Our way of life is somewhat simpler on Eden. There are some facets of your culture I do envy."

"Oh?" she replied, "Is that so?" Her curiosity had been piqued, and she hoped he would elaborate further. She had previously thought that everyone from Eden was a brainwashed, religious simpleton, but Ambassador Harris fit right in here on Ymir.

"Indeed," he answered, "In fact I would very much like to continue this conversation, perhaps somewhere less… public." She took his meaning, and it further intrigued her. He wanted to talk to her somewhere away from prying eyes and ears. Now this was politics, and she was happy to indulge him.

"Of course," she answered, smiling easily. "Please, right this way." She took his proffered arm, and he escorted her as she led him away to one of the more private rooms of the building. She shut the door carefully behind them, and then took a seat. All of her attention was focused on what he had to say.

He paced back and forth for a moment, collecting his thoughts before he began. "The more time I spend here," he told her, "the more discontented I am with the situation on Eden."

How so? she wondered. *What is he getting at, and why is he bringing this to me?*

"As I'm sure you are aware, Eden is a theocracy. The priests rule over the people absolutely, with no challenge to their fitness to govern. They hold every high office, with the sole exception of my post. The only reason I was even able to secure the role of ambassador is that they themselves refuse to leave Eden." He paused, considering his next words.

"Frankly, as I'm sure you're aware, all of their religious talk is a load of tripe." Victoria was surprised to hear his admission. This was interesting indeed. She waited for him to continue.

"I can't stand the thought of those old, bungling fools trying to run an entire world. They're so caught up in their own dreck that I wouldn't be surprised if they've all fallen for it themselves. Eden needs a better leader, someone moral and rational, who can make decisions without burning incense or flailing around speaking made up languages, who can hold the public's trust without relying on phony religious propaganda."

Now, Victoria understood exactly where he was going with this, and why he had come to her of all people. Surely enough, he continued: "As the only government official who does not buy into that garbage, I am uniquely placed to challenge their rule, however, I would need the support and resources of someone influential. Naturally I would make it worth their while."

Ambassador Harris turned to face her, and got right to the point. "Your father is the most prominent and influential member of the Ymir council. Obviously, I can't approach him openly about a matter such as this, so I'm asking you to intercede on my behalf. I can promise his efforts in this regard will be rewarded once we succeed." He waited expectantly for her response. Victoria mulled the idea over. The ambassador was hopelessly optimistic if he thought an operation of this magnitude would be easy, but the idea had enough merit that her political genes were intrigued. She couldn't resist. She wanted to hear more.

"Alright," she answered, "but my father is a practical man, I'm going to need details and a plan of action before he'll commit to anything."

"Of course," Ambassador Harris smiled. "Thank you for granting me this opportunity. It is a pleasure to be working with you." He bowed graciously as he spoke.

No ambassador, she thought to herself, the wheels in her head already turning. *The pleasure is all mine.*

It was quite late when Victoria finally staggered back through the door to her quarters on the military base. She managed to change out of her dress uniform before slumping onto the bed. She was physically exhausted but her mind was wide awake.

This was a perfect opportunity for her! She would work with the ambassador and put together a feasible plan of action to present to her father. He would sign off on it, and she would finally get the recognition she deserved. A strong alliance between Eden and Ymir, and it would be thanks to her efforts. Finally, she had found the opportunity she had been searching for.

Chapter 2

Remedial class, what a pain, Alex thought as he slouched in his desk listening to the instructor ramble on. Apparently, their performance on the sim had convinced the instructors that the cadets needed the gravity of the situation pounded into their heads again, so that they understood exactly what a failed mission meant. This resulted in a lengthy rundown of the colony's entire history. Again. In detail. The fact that any of the cadets could likely recite the whole lecture from memory was, apparently, irrelevant.

The basic rundown started with *Spirit of Hope,* the colony ship that brought humanity here to the Delta Pavonis system, one hundred years ago. The passengers aboard *Spirit of Hope* had established a colony on the planet Pavonis Prime, and everything seemed to be going well. Gravity and atmospheric composition were very close to those of Earth, and the plants they had carried with them adapted to the alien soil with only minor genetic tweaks. The discovery of a world so similar to the one they had left behind was almost miraculous. Pavonis Prime's orbit was slightly farther from its star, resulting in a 395 day year, but the slightly greater warmth of its sun balanced out its temperature.

Then, fifty years in, the settlers uncovered a strange artifact while mining, which seemed to suggest some form of alien civilization had existed there, though there was no evidence of any currently living on the planet, or anywhere else in the system. Shortly after that, the artificially intelligent robots which the colonists had used extensively, both in the construction of the colony, and in its day to day operations, went mad. There was no other way to describe it. Analysis of units retrieved intact yielded no logical explanation. Then, the robots turned hostile toward the colonists, quickly driving them offworld.

That brought things to the current situation. Humanity now clung to life on Pavonis Prime's three moons. Alex had been born here. This cold, unforgiving ball of ice known as Ymir was the only home he'd ever had. Now it was his responsibility to defend it from attacks launched off the planet they orbited. This tenuous grip on survival was Alex's reality, he was fully aware of it, and he was sick and tired of hearing about it. So he had to deal with the mess his grandparents generation had unleashed? Fine.

Next came the video. It was always the same one. There wasn't much surviving footage capturing the events of the war's beginning. This was the only full video that had been edited together, and Alex had seen it countless times. The instructors believed showing the gruesome events would somehow spur the cadets to greater effort, but after so many viewings, Alex and the others were essentially immune to it. Not even Victoria bothered to act like she was paying attention.

The screen in front of the room lit up as the video began, showing the war-torn outskirts of a large city. A ragged line of human troops desperately fought to hold off an advancing wave of machines as the civilians fled. The soldiers fought valiantly, but the machines did not waver. For every one that fell, another took its place. It wasn't long before the soldiers were overwhelmed by the advancing tide of hostile robots.

Then there was nothing between the machines and the fleeing civilians. Without hesitation they continued their advance, firing into the panicking crowd indiscriminately. There, the video ended.

"This is the threat we face." The lecturer spoke. "There is no mercy from the machines. We must remain ever vigilant and stand fast to defend our world." He continued to ramble on for some time after this.

Just give it a rest, Alex attempted to will the instructor to finish his lecture so they could leave. To his surprise, the instructor picked that moment to begin wrapping up his speech. "That is all for today, class dismissed." Alex pondered the situation for a moment. *Did I just...? Nah, don't be stupid, Alex. Just be glad it's over.* He shook his head to drive away the thought, and exited the classroom. After a moment's reflection, he veered from his auto-piloted course to the barracks, back toward the simulator facility. He might as well get in some practice while he was here. It wasn't like he had anything else pressing to do. He checked in at the front desk of the facility, and was assigned a vacant machine. The simulators were sleek, white pods shaped like elongated eggs lying on their sides, with shiny, black canopy bubbles rising from their tops. The pods were mounted to a frame capable of rotating them freely on all three axes. Alex made his way over to his assigned pod and climbed up the ladder with a practiced ease. Settling in, he hit the switch to close the canopy, and waited for his chosen scenario to start. He had picked a solo mission, since he wasn't feeling particularly social at the moment.

The viewscreen came to life before him, and the mission began. With a roar from his engines, he launched from the familiar hangar bay, built into the side of the crater inside which sat his colony, out into the brilliant, blue landscape of Ymir. The vast majority of the moon's surface was covered in a thick sheet of ice, and the landscape around the colony was no exception. During the day, anyone outside needed protective eyewear to counter the harsh glare of reflected light off the omnipresent ice. The cluster of structures that was Nifelheim, huddled beneath a large, tinted dome, which protected the colony from the unforgiving elements, receded behind him. They marked humanity's only foothold in this inhospitable place, and looked so vulnerable from outside. Alex focused his attention on the mission objectives. Most scenarios were variations on the same theme: engage incoming hostiles and eliminate them before they reach the colony. Base defense was their entire purpose. Alex could see the incoming ships now, minimalist models refined by their AI designers, with data from hundreds of encounters with their human opponents. These particular vessels were dropships loaded with ground troops ready to deploy and advance on Nifelheim. A ground assault would be disastrous, since all the defenses were devoted to anti-air weaponry. Ymir didn't have the resources to cover both fronts. He had to take the ships out before they landed. Alex flicked his targeting reticule to the first silvery egg-shaped vessel, held his breath, and depressed the trigger. Lances of angry, red light connected with the ship, and it burst in a cloud of flame. The shockwave rattled his ship. This fight was taking place within the atmosphere, making it all the more urgent. The moon's atmosphere, and Earth-like gravity, despite its small size, still baffled scientists, though many colonists, Alex included, pointed to the evidence of an alien presence as a possible explanation. He shook his head, driving away the distraction. He had to force himself to stay focused. Simulation or no, he couldn't afford to get distracted.

The other dropships were already opening up with their own salvos, forcing him to roll out of their lane of fire. He lined up with a second ship and fired again, leaving a deep gash along its side. Diving to avoid bolts from the third vessel, he came around to fire again. This time his target came apart in a satisfying explosion. Turning his full attention to the last ship, he caught one of its engines. Smoke pouring from it, the ship's nose came down, putting it on a collision course with the ground. As he was lining up a second shot, the simulator pod suddenly shook wildly, and a chorus of alarms began blaring. He had been hit from behind. A robotic fighter, sleek and deadly, shot past. It hadn't been present when he first engaged, so it must have joined the skirmish while he was focused on the other ships. His fighter was a wreck, now on its own inevitable journey toward the ground below. With a sigh of frustration, Alex hit the ejection switch, opening the canopy of the pod.

The results were not good. The last ship he had shot down was able to deploy its troops. Half the city's population wiped out. Clearly, Alex decided, he needed more time in the sims. His ratings were going to take a hit for this. Any simulator course a cadet participated in, whether assigned by the instructors or as voluntary practice on their own time, was logged, weighted, and averaged into the pilot's performance rating. *Well,* he thought, *it can't be helped now.* He headed back toward the dorms to shower off and relax a bit before the next mind numbing remedial course began.

# # #

Victoria watched as Alex left the sim facility. When she had first spotted him, she had briefly considered calling out to him, but had decided against it. He had been in kind of a funk since the tongue-lashing they had received after the last exam scenario. She slipped her own flight helmet off and shook her head to let her hair fall back into order. Sliding down the metal ladder with practiced ease, she approached a nearby vending machine and ordered a cold drink. While sipping it, she reflected on the events of the day of the exam. When Alex had refused her lunch offer. When she had found her father waiting for her. When the ambassador proposed a government upheaval. Life was crazy right now, but she could handle it. She always had before.

Chapter 3

Alert sirens pierced the air, and Alex bolted upright in his bed. The shrill alarms signaled an imminent attack. A *real* attack. He glanced over to George, who was similarly up and alert. Their eyes met for a moment, and then they both jumped out of their beds and scrambled to change into their flight suits before racing out the door. This was the first real attack since they had entered the academy, but due to monthly drills they knew the standard procedure: dress up and go to the briefing room to observe the battle on the tactical screens.

Alex stumbled breathlessly into the briefing room a few minutes later. Most of the other pilots were assembled already and the admiral had begun the briefing. Alex and George quietly took a place in the back, listening intently.

"This is the largest attacking force we've ever faced," Admiral Anderson was explaining. "We will need every ship we can muster to be airborne." His eyes swept over the assembled pilots. "That includes you cadets. We do not have enough veteran pilots for this operation, so this will be your first real engagement." Alex's heart was pounding in his chest now. There was no way he was ready for this, but what choice did he have?

"It is no exaggeration to say that the survival of this colony hinges on this battle," the admiral continued. "We're all counting on you. Dismissed."

Alex began his preflight checklist while settling into the cockpit seat of a real *Valkyrie*-class starfighter. This was no simulation. It was the real deal. Lives were at stake. Alex tried to force those thoughts out of his head as he prepared to launch. The cadets had been broken into groups and assigned experienced pilots as commanders. Alex, George, and a few other cadets were flying under Lt. Martinez. The others were similarly distributed among the other squadrons.

"Just stick close and follow my orders and we'll come out of this alive," Martinez assured them. "Rookie with the least kills buys us a round when we get back!" The other vets voiced their approval at that, and Alex couldn't help but smile, the tension drained to a manageable level.

They were green-lighted for launch, and Alex was shoved back into his seat as his fighter leapt out of the hangar and into the dazzling glacial fields of Ymir. Alex pulled back on his flight stick, pointing his ship away from the brilliant blue ice and toward the dark expanse of space above. A field of tiny specks of light stood out slightly brighter than the surrounding stars. Alex's heart sank at the number of them. These were their targets, and there were far more of them than there were of the small fleet of human ships opposing them.

The next moment, he lost the luxury of thinking. Angry, red lances speared out from the approaching enemies, seeking to tear the defenders apart. Confusion reigned unchecked across the com channels. The distance was still too great to engage, and the pilots were caught off-guard. At least, most of them were.

"All squads, evasive maneuvers, now!" Victoria's tone rang out across the com, cutting through the milieu of voices. "Close and engage the enemy." There was no dissent. No one questioned her authority. The defending forces fell back into a semblance of order and pressed through the storm, taking some losses, but far fewer than they might have.

# # #

Victoria hadn't planned on this. Somehow, she was now running the entire battle. Thanks to the humiliating simulated defeat, which still bothered her, she had not been caught off-guard by the early salvo. When everything started falling apart around her, she had responded without thinking. She was used to leading exercises with the other cadets, so it was natural for her to take charge. The problem was that it had worked, and everyone was now looking to her to pull this off. Everyone. Ground base had even transferred command priority to her fighter's com system. Her orders would now show up on all squadrons' screens. So be it.

"Squad one, engage their fighter screen and take it out; you don't have the firepower to open up those dropships. Squad two, you have the left flank. Squad three, the right. Squad four, we're headed straight up the middle. The other squadron leaders acknowledged, to her continued incredulity, and the defenders pressed forward to meet their adversaries.

# # #

Alex, in squad two, lined up the first target in his sights as he watched the range count down toward his weapons' maximum effective distance. In a twist of fate, the veteran pilots had been shaken worse by this turn of events than the cadets, and their roles were now seemingly reversed. Lieutenant Martinez had been one of the casualties of the first volley. Alex felt sick to his stomach, but he couldn't afford to mourn the dead now. His ship's computer sounded a tone notifying him that his target was now within range. He depressed the trigger, finally able to retaliate. Deep welts appeared in the ship's silvery exterior, and then a silent explosion blossomed within it, bursting it like a balloon. Alex immediately turned his attention to the next target. The battle raged furiously, and, with Victoria now calling the shots, it seemed like the defenders actually had the upper hand. Far more AI ships had been destroyed than human fighters, but the defenders were running out of time. The AI dropships had not slowed their approach at all during the battle, and those that remained were now dangerously close to Ymir's atmosphere, apparently content to sacrifice the bulk of their fleet in order to reach their target. Alex brought his fighter to bear on a dropship already glowing with the heat of atmospheric reentry. His first shots went wide as the dropship dove into a sharper descent toward the icy ground below, but his next volley was on-target, coring through one of the vessel's engines. Smoking and running on only three thrusters now, the ship dropped like a rock, descending out of control toward the surface. Alex continued to pursue it, remembering all too well the results of the simulation during which he had allowed a single damaged ship to reach the surface. As he was lining up another shot, a blinding light filled his cockpit followed by blackness.

He came to moments later, the shrill blaring of alarms lancing through his skull. He'd been hit from behind, and was falling rapidly. The controls were barely responsive. He couldn't avoid crashing, only soften the impact somewhat. The ship he'd disabled slammed down a few dozen meters off his left wing, and the shockwave threw him spinning sideways into the outer wall of the crater, inside which the only home he'd ever known lay nestled. Darkness took him again.

When he snapped awake this time, his head felt like it was splitting open, and he tasted blood, but otherwise he seemed to be intact. He glanced up to see a face staring through the cockpit canopy at him. Cold steel, with two red, glowing orbs where a human's eyes would be. It lacked any capacity for displaying emotion. It had a roughly humanoid build, but looked gaunt and skeletal. Its limbs were more slender than a person's, but Alex knew they were still powerful. None of the robots the colonists had encountered were ever painted. Aesthetics were lost on them. It raised one arm, purposefully and deliberately, and then slammed its fist into the canopy. The canopy held, but surely would not last long under such punishment. Alex scrambled to find the pistol stored in the fighter's cockpit, managed to draw it, and brought it to bear on his assailant. The robot didn't react to the weapon at all, drawing its arm back yet again, and slamming it once more into the canopy. This time, a fine spider web of cracks spread across it. Alex fired. The weapon's blast speared through the canopy, melting a neat hole, and pierced the robot's forehead. The light in its eyes flickered out, and it slumped to the right and slipped off the fighter. Alex breathed a sigh of relief.

The very next moment, however, the fighter shook from an even stronger impact. Alex hit the release for the restraints, and pushed open the battered remains of the canopy. The robot responsible for this new disturbance was the same steely silver color as the first, and bore the same brilliant ruby eyes, but the similarities ended there. This one was as large as his ship, with massive arms and squat legs. It reminded him of images of gorillas taken long ago on Earth. The bot raised its arm again, and Alex hastily leapt clear. The second blow came down directly on the cockpit, crushing it. The great metal ape turned its attention to him now. It raised its other arm, and the flash of a built-in weapon's discharge was predicated by a large patch of ice to Alex's left evaporating instantly in a cloud of steam. He was paralyzed before the massive machine, unable to will himself to move as it carefully adjusted its aim. Alex clenched his eyes shut expecting the end. A brilliant flash pierced the thin veil of his eyelids, then nothing.

Nothing? No pain? No heat? He was seemingly still intact. He opened his eyes to see a shimmering barrier separating him from the bot. He had no time to process this strange turn of events, as the next moment, hellfire rained from above, incinerating his antagonist. A *Valkyrie*-class fighter arced away from its strafing run and banked to come in for a landing approach. Someone had followed him when he went down.

More robots were lumbering toward him. Their carapaces were painfully bright, gleaming in the combined light of the sun above and the reflective ice below. His pistol was gone. In his haste to exit his fighter, he had left it behind. He watched helplessly, terror building inside him, as they relentlessly pressed closer with each step. In desperation, his mind raced. *Just leave me alone!* it screamed. *Go away!* The thought echoed within his skull with the force of an explosion.

The bots then shook and convulsed as if caught in a seizure. One of the nearest machines was thrown violently sideways, a huge, crumpled dent in its side as if it had been struck by some invisible assailant. The head of a second automaton crumpled and imploded. Alex could not understand what was happening, or why his body, while full of adrenaline, now felt overtaxed as if he had just run a marathon. All around him, the robots fell, reacting to blows he could not see. In mere moments, the entire force lay silently on the ground, torn apart by a process he couldn't comprehend. Alex felt very tired, and offered little resistance as darkness came to claim him for the third time that day. Just as he was succumbing, he saw a lone, human figure running toward him, concern and fear etched into its face, the mouth moving, speaking words he could no longer hear.

# # #

Alex's eyes snapped open to reveal a harsh, white ceiling above him. "It's about time you woke up," a familiar voice remarked. He turned his head to see Victoria seated next to his bed. Her eyes brightened to see him awake, surprising him. Since when was she concerned what happened to him? How long had she been there, waiting? The day's earlier events came back to him in a rush and he had to know everything. "What about the battle?" he asked. "What happened?"

"We took heavy losses, but we held out," Victoria assured him. "The attackers were completely destroyed." Then she continued: "Apparently they're making me out to be some kind of hero for stepping in like that and taking charge. I was expecting a court martial over it."

She turned away for a moment, as if deliberating over what she was about to say. "I saw you go down, and as soon as I had a chance, I went after you… to clear out the bots, naturally." She continued quickly. "I was the one who took out that hulking monstrosity that had you pinned." Another pause. "I was the one who found you."

Everything came rushing back: his desperate struggle after he was shot down and the strange experience with the robots. What was she getting at? Was she suggesting he had been responsible for that? His mind was still groggy. "I'm not sure I understand what you're saying..." he said slowly.

"I did some digging," Victoria replied. "I would not have been satisfied until I got to the bottom of this." She stood and walked to the door, opening it. His parents stood outside. Of course they were here, but what did they have to do with whatever Victoria was talking about, and why hadn't they been waiting beside his bed instead of Victoria? They reluctantly walked into the room and stood awkwardly, not making eye contact. Victoria addressed him again. "Your test turned up positive, but your parents begged and pleaded, and offered quite a sum of money for the testers to look the other way. Luckily for them, the officer present was more than happy to agree." His parents still wouldn't make eye contact.

Test? What was she saying? What officer? Why were his parents reacting like this? Then, in one terrible instant, everything snapped together clearly. Victoria was talking about the psionics test given to infants. They were telling him he was one of the gifted.

"We just..." his mother began quietly, "we just wanted to do what we thought was best for you." His father placed his hand on her arm and squeezed reassuringly. They still would not meet his eyes.

"You wanted what was best for me, or what was best for you?" Alex retorted. He didn't really think he'd have wanted to grow up in the research center, but he was still furious that they had never told him any of this.

"We'd heard things about that place," his father replied. "None of them pleasant. We wanted to spare you that. We've seen those *things* walking about sometimes. It's like they aren't even human."

"I'm not going to report any of this," Victoria assured them, then turned to look Alex in the eye, "but you owe me one for this, Alex." He didn't know what she had in mind, but he was sure he was not going to like it. If she was choosing to let him go like this, it could only mean this favor was more valuable to her than the reward for turning him in, and that she was convinced that he would have refused her without this leverage.

His parents left shortly afterward, at Victoria's promptings to allow him to get some rest. She followed them out, but hesitated at the door, then finally left without another word to him. He lay back on the bed, but the revelations of the day prevented him from sleeping. It would have been far better to never have found out. He was sure he'd now live the rest of his life fearing the threat of discovery. What would George and the others think if they knew? Would they report him if they found out? Doubt and speculation plagued him through the night.

Chapter 4

Alex was discharged from the hospital the next day. Reluctantly, he stepped through the front door, exchanging the temporary safe haven for the far more complicated world outside. How fortunate for him to be released just in time to attend the ceremony Councilman Barrett had arranged for his daughter and the other cadets who had fought to defend the colony. A week ago, Alex would have been elated to be honored like this, but with the revelations of yesterday, being in the spotlight was the last thing he wanted. It wasn't simple paranoia. He had every right to be concerned. He shuddered as he recalled the nightmare that had tormented him last night.

Alex had found himself sitting in the familiar classroom as the instructor was wrapping up for the day. His friends had approached his desk after class ended, and he could feel their eyes cutting through him, uncovering what he was trying desperately to hide. They had recoiled in disgust. George's face contorted into a grimace. Then they began to back away. He had reached out to them, desperate to call them back. Instead, they began to writhe in pain, as their bodies contorted, limbs snapping, ribs cracking, and worst of all their accusing eyes meeting his. He was killing them. *No!* He could only watch helplessly unable to stop it. Then, he had snapped awake covered in sweat.

Was something like that possible? He had no idea what his hidden abilities could actually do, or how he could even control them. Any time he had used them had been a reflexive action. Maybe it would be better to turn himself over after all. Conflicted, he continued on his way to the city center where the assembly was taking place. He could see the crowd gathering ahead of him. Several thousand colonists, likely. To Alex it was a huge crowd. There were a few million people living on each of the three moons. Accounts of billions of people living back on Earth were beyond his comprehension.

He made his way to the rear entrance of the building and slipped inside. He found the room where the other cadets were situated and moved to join them. Victoria seemed to catch his eye as he entered, but looked away quickly, wearing her usual unreadable mask.

"Nothing but the best for my daughter," George began to say, hands on hips and chest puffed out, impersonating Victoria's father. Many of the gathered cadets attempted to stifle their laughter with varying degrees of success.

"This isn't about me," Victoria interrupted, glaring at George. "It's a ceremony honoring all of us, *and*," she continued, "to honor everyone we lost." The humor was sucked out of the air in an instant at the reminder. Half of their classmates and many veteran pilots hadn't made it. Alex surveyed his surviving friends and classmates, all too aware how small the group seemed now. The conversation terminated awkwardly as the cadets all turned inward to reflect on and grieve the loss of so many. An aide popped her head through the doorway to inform them that the ceremony would soon start, asking them to follow her. They shuffled out after her, solemnly and silently.

The curtain before them parted, revealing the sea of faces before them. Harsh light poured into their eyes and made the stage uncomfortably warm in their dress uniforms. Councilman Barrett stood center-stage behind a podium, with the cadets seated behind and to his right. He gripped the edges of the podium and addressed the assembled crowd.

"Fellow citizens," he began, "we come together today to recognize the valor of our young men and women in uniform who fought bravely this week to protect our colony from those who would do us harm. It is because of their courage in the face of overwhelming odds that we are standing here today." Applause broke out at that and it was a moment before he could speak again.

"This victory was not won without great cost," he continued, and the crowd sobered considerably. "We gather here both to recognize the efforts of the living, and honor the sacrifice of those who died that day. We begin with the cadets you see assembled before you." He half turned toward them. "Through their actions, they have more than proven themselves in real combat. Therefore, as of this day, they are cadets no longer, and will immediately be welcomed as full-fledged pilots in our armed forces." A buzz of excitement and surprise ran through the assembled cadets. Alex turned to see George grinning ear to ear. The assembled cadets were called forward, one at a time. As each stepped forward to receive a signed certificate of graduation and shake the councilman's hand, thunderous applause rose from the gathered crowd. Alex strode across the stage purposefully as his name was called. The councilman, who Alex had met several times before since he was a friend of Victoria's, smiled warmly as he handed him the graduation paper and firmly shook his hand.

Once all the cadets had been recognized, Marcus Barrett turned to address the crowd again, "Now, let us end today by remembering those fine men and women who gave their lives in our defense." The large screen mounted on the wall behind him lit up, displaying the names and faces of those killed in action. Not a single sound could be heard during the solemn presentation. It was especially hard for them to see this. The loss was still so recent, and he and the other cadets had grown up alongside these people their whole lives. Many had had far more promising futures than he, and none of them deserved to die so young. Letters of condolence would be mailed to parents, and funerals would be held. Alex didn't know what consolation those families would be able to draw from that, but it usually seemed to do some good.

After a short speech from the councilman to end on, the ceremony was over. The gathered colonists gradually dispersed, returning to their everyday lives. *How many will have completely forgotten the week's events within a few days?* Alex wondered. Shaking his head, he began to walk back to the dormitory. They had the day off tomorrow, and many cadets were headed home to visit their families. Alex had no intention of doing so. He still wasn't ready to see them after what had happened at the hospital. He reached the dormitory, made his way down the hall to his room, and let himself fall face first onto the bed, not even bothering to change out of his stiff, formal uniform. He lay there for quite some time before sleep finally took him.

# # #

The ceremony had ended, but Victoria knew she would not be able to leave for quite some time. Her father, having performed for the masses, was now working his magic on the press. He was certain to play up her role in the battle, and their family's heroic sacrifice and dedication in allowing her to serve. How like him to try to take this from her. It had been *her* decision to enlist and serve in the first place. It was a good way to build a name for herself and establish an identity separate from his, outside his shadow. He had agreed to the idea, but merely as a means to bolster his approval ratings, helping him to win a landslide reelection. He was like a parasite, turning the accomplishments of others, her, his advisors, or anyone else to his gain. If she was ever to be acknowledged as something other than an extension of him, she needed to put an end to that. She decided then and there not to tell him anything about Ambassador Harris' request. She wouldn't allow him to take that opportunity for himself.

She took a moment to compose herself, then opened the door and pushed through the throng of reporters. Her father already had them wrapped around his finger. "Ah, Victoria," he smiled, "the hero of the hour. I was just explaining how you snatched victory from the jaws of defeat out there." He turned to the crowd of journalists before him and winked. "Just like a Barrett to take charge when the chips are down!" They ate it up, laughter filling the room. Victoria forced a warm smile as she crossed over to him, but inwardly she seethed. Just as she'd expected, he was twisting this. It wasn't her accomplishment now. It was Barrett quality shining through. She promised herself that this would be the last time he ever took anything from her.

Chapter 5

Victoria continued to pace, which was quite uncharacteristic of her. It was 4 in the morning—all colonies followed a 24 hour Earth day—and she hadn't slept a moment. The aftermath of the ceremony kept replaying through her mind. Curse her father.

Her thoughts turned again to Ambassador Harris and her plans, but one thing was stubbornly holding her back. *Alex.* Her heart hurt to think about him. She knew what he would probably think of what she intended to do. If she continued down this path it could tear them apart irreparably. She knew it, and so she hesitated, unable to commit one way or the other.

Two paths lay ahead of her, on one she saw herself with Alex, happy together with him. Oblivious as he was, she was sure she could win him over. On the other path she saw her road to power. She would play along with the Ambassador until she no longer needed him, then use him as a springboard to assume power, not for her sake, but for the sake of the people. Could she pull them both off? Should she try?

Her father's words echoed through her mind. "Always put the people first," he had lectured her. Back when he had been younger, more idealistic. She took those words to heart. Either way she couldn't afford to waste any time.

# # #

"You need me for what, exactly?" Alex wanted to know, trying to shake off the last traces of sleep. Typical that Victoria would call first thing in the morning, demanding what little free time he had.

"I need you to accompany me to meet Ambassador Harris. I can't meet him without some kind of escort," Victoria explained patiently.

"Can't your father arrange one for you?" Alex pressed on. He knew it was pointless to raise objections but felt obligated to do so anyway. One way or another he would inevitably be dragged into this. Whatever Victoria wanted, she was bound to get it one way or another.

"Ordinarily yes, of course, but I want you this time. We need to talk afterwards. I'm heading to class now. Be ready for me when it's over." The line went dead.

Alex sighed. Somehow, it always turned out like this. Victoria ended up dragging him along on some errand or another whether he liked it or not. He also couldn't ignore the very real threat of her turning him in if he didn't oblige her. She had him right where she wanted him. He reluctantly rolled out of bed and began preparing for whatever had caught her interest this time.

"Duty calls?" George joked from his bunk across the room, having woken up during the call.

"Oh shut up," Alex wasn't in the mood for his teasing right now. George just grinned, annoying Alex even more.

# # #

Alex sat in the classroom where he had spent so much time over the past year. This would be the last time he sat here in these chairs. They had been called here for one last session after their graduation from the academy. The unorthodox nature of their ascension to full military personnel had spurred the impromptu session.

Commander Prescott made his way to the lectern at the front of the room. Alex did a double take when he first saw the man. He scarcely recognized him. The sharp, stern expression was gone from his face. Previously, he had always stood tall—ramrod straight. Now, however, he was stooped and seemed far shorter. All of the fire had gone out of the man. He seemed a mere husk of his former self. What had happened? What hardship could force a man to change so much? Alex shot a look to George, but he simply shrugged. No one knew what was going on.

Prescott reached the lectern and coughed to clear his throat. With some effort, he began to speak. "As you all know, from this day forward, you are no longer cadets. You have graduated to full military service. This extraordinary measure was taken because of our great need. It is our hope that your time spent here will serve you well in the future, as you serve to defend our colony."

He paused here, and it seemed to take a great effort to continue. "Many fine men and women were lost to us. My son was one of them." This then was the cause of the radical transformation the professor had undergone. "Let us hope that you are ready to fill the gaps left by their sacrifice." He swept his eyes across his former students. This time, no one flinched under his gaze; the fire had been extinguished from his eyes. He turned and left the room without another word.

# # #

"Where exactly are we headed?" Alex asked, as he walked alongside Victoria, headed toward the city proper. "Why are you meeting the Eden colony ambassador, anyway?"

"We're going to the psychic research center." Victoria replied. "There are several subjects from Eden colony there, so he has a right to inspect the facility. The way they practically worship gifted on Eden, visits like this go a long way to keep positive relations between colonies, and ensure their continuing support of the project."

That seemed logical to Alex. Very few people were allowed entrance to the facility so it was a topic of much speculation to most citizens of Ymir. However, there was a more pressing concern for Alex himself. "Are you mad?" he practically shouted at her. "If I go in there, there's no telling if I ever come back out! If they find out what I am, I'll spend the rest of my life in there!"

Victoria regarded him coolly. "As far as anyone knows, there's never been a case of someone not being detected and reported. They have no reason at all to suspect their visitors of secretly being psychic. You're smarter than this, Alex Morris. There's no reason for you to become paranoid."

She was right. He knew she was, but somehow that didn't help much. They made their way across the city toward the center in silence. Alex could see the large, grey building looming in the distance. It stood in stark contrast to the other buildings nearby. Its most striking feature was its complete lack of windows, which made perfect sense for this kind of facility, due to the sensitive nature of the research conducted there.

Ambassador Harris was waiting for them outside, near the entrance of the building. Alex stood uncomfortably as Victoria exchanged pleasantries with the ambassador and his entourage. Finally, the group began moving toward the building. A security checkpoint was set up just inside the entrance. While Victoria and Ambassador Harris checked in, Alex took in his first glimpse of the research center's interior. The walls and ceiling were stark white with a plain, grey carpet covering the floor. The sterile illumination of fluorescent lights lit the interior. The building's architect certainly wasn't out to impress anyone. A long hallway led to a bank of elevators, and past that were numerous, plain wooden doors with small, numbered metal plaques as the only clues as to their contents.

After they had been scanned and frisked to the security officers' satisfaction, they were escorted to the elevators. Once everyone was inside, the guard allowed the machine to scan his retina, then wordlessly selected a floor. The elevator descended in silence for several minutes, and Alex could only guess how far beneath the surface they were when the doors opened again. They stepped out into a hallway identical to the one they had left far above them on the surface.

A woman in a standard white lab coat stood waiting for them. "I'm Dr. Mercer," she began, "I'll be your guide for the duration of your visit." There was a hint of disapproval and resentment in her voice, suggesting she viewed this as a gross misallocation of her time. "We currently have six test subjects from the Eden colony," she continued as they made their way down the hall. "Four male, and two female. Three of them are currently unavailable as they are in the middle of critical tests. If you need to see them you will have to return at a later date." She turned to face the ambassador.

"I understand," the ambassador replied, smiling disarmingly. "Once I've made my report, I'll arrange another visit if my superiors think it is warranted." Dr. Mercer nodded curtly, annoyed-but-satisfied with that and turned her attention forward again.

"Here is the dormitory facility for our test subjects," she waved toward a door on the left marked 706. "One moment." The door scanner accepted her retinal pattern and moments later they were inside. "I'll call for them to be brought out," the doctor informed them. "Please wait here." She strode purposefully to the room's desk a short distance away.

This room matched the drab design style of the rest of the facility. It was hard to think of it as any kind of living space. Two hallways branched off the main room, with rows of identical doors spread along them. Wings for male and female residents, Alex guessed. The man stationed behind the desk had headed down one of the corridors after a brief conversation with Dr. Mercer, and after a short wait he returned with two boys, both younger than Alex. Shortly after that he returned with a girl who looked to be around Alex and Victoria's age.

All three of them wore an outfit similar to a hospital gown as well as the iconic helmets synonymous with the gifted. Dr. Mercer explained that the helmets were, in fact, for the protection of the guests rather than the children themselves. Gifted children occasionally had difficulty controlling their abilities, and it wouldn't do to have a VIP injured or killed by an accident. Ambassador Harris busied himself interrogating Dr. Mercer about the experiments and the level of care the subjects received, with Victoria listening intently next to him. Alex was left to stand around, bored, wishing the whole thing was over with. It was then that he noticed the girl staring directly at him. Well, he couldn't exactly call it staring with her eyes covered, but he couldn't explain it any other way. Several minutes passed uncomfortably for him and still she was unmistakably focused on him. Why he of all people attracted her attention was beyond him, and now more than ever he wanted to put this whole thing behind him.

# # #

"A demonstration perhaps would be nice," the ambassador was saying. "Some concrete results for my superiors to assure them that this program is truly worthwhile." Victoria could read between the lines of his request easily enough. Eden colony was looking for some excuse to pull its prized gifted out of this joint project, and if the center didn't oblige his request he would be delivering just the excuse needed.

"Of course," Dr. Mercer replied, clearly annoyed by the extension to their visit. "Right this way." She led them back to the elevator, down again to another larger room, this time with thick steel doors. "Subject 173," she addressed one of the boys, "you will provide the demonstration." Wordlessly, the boy walked to the steel examination chair in the center of the room and sat down. "This way please," the doctor directed them through a small door to an observation room with a large, one-way observation window. As they walked, Victoria bristled with an unfamiliar and uncomfortable emotion. The female test subject was paying extremely close attention to Alex. She forced herself to shake it off, and turned to watch the test that had begun.

# # #

This, at least, was more interesting than the rest of the tour, Alex conceded to himself. The test had begun with some basic telepathy and telekinesis demonstrations. Mind reading and levitating small objects were apparently basic skills for the children here. He watched intently as the boy now moved on to deflecting projectiles that were being launched toward him. Soft foam-rubber balls were fired out of a tube toward him at various speeds and trajectories. As they approached the boy, the balls invariably recoiled and bounced away. A faint ripple of energy in the air, that he may in fact be imagining, gave the only visual hint as to what was happening. The boy was repelling them with his abilities. Alex was caught up in the experiments, so he was startled when a voice whispered in his ear.

"You're here. I told them you would come." Alex turned to see the girl was now standing uncomfortably close, somehow meeting his eyes from behind the helmet.

"I have no idea what you're talking about," he insisted. Could she tell somehow? He felt in very real danger here. If this girl reported him to Dr. Mercer, and the doctor believed her, then this would be the end right here.

"Where is your helmet?" she queried him, removing any doubt that she knew exactly what he was. She cocked her head quizzically, as if pondering her own question. She stood quietly staring at him, waiting patiently for him to answer.

"I don't need one," he assured her, "I'm not like you. You're mistaken. I'm normal, like the doctors." He glanced toward Dr. Mercer as he said this, but she was caught up in her demonstration and had not noticed their conversation. He desperately wanted to get out of here and hoped fervently that the demonstration would not last much longer.

The girl continued to stare at him. She gave no sign as to whether she had understood, or even heard his response. Seconds passed like hours as he tried to ignore her stare and pretended to be interested in the demonstration.

At last, the test ended and the time came to leave. Dr. Mercer assigned a security officer to escort them out while she led the children back to their dormitory. The girl continued staring at Alex the entire time, until they were finally out of sight. The trip back to the surface and out of the research center was uneventful. Victoria and Ambassador Harris exchanged goodbyes, and then it was just the two of them.

"Come on," Victoria said, "there's a lot to talk about." He followed without complaint as she led him somewhere they could talk privately.

# # #

Alex and Victoria had settled on a small cafe near the city center, taking a table outside and placing an order for some drinks. Once the waitress had departed after delivering their order, Victoria began to explain the ambassador's grand scheme to him. Alex listened incredulously as she calmly laid out the treasonous plan as if it were perfectly normal. This was what she wanted to talk to him about? Had she lost her mind? His face must have betrayed something because she stopped midsentence, frowning.

"I take it you don't approve," she accused him, "but it would be foolish to pass up an opportunity like this."

"What opportunity?" Alex blurted out, "you're only sixteen for God's sake and you're plotting treason! This is crazy." *When did she go off the deep end?* he asked himself. He hadn't noticed anything out of the ordinary over the previous few months. She had apparently just snapped. It seemed that she wasn't satisfied with her life anymore, and now she was taking rather drastic action as a result.

Her eyes flashed angrily. "You don't think I can pull this off? If we were talking about this colony or Adar, maybe not," she conceded, "but those superstitious fools will just eat this up. The ambassador himself is convinced of it or we wouldn't be talking about it in the first place."

"So what was the point of this excursion then?" Alex asked.

"We wanted a chance to pick out our messiah. We were evaluating the candidates. Once we've decided, the ambassador will pressure them to release that one gifted to return to Eden with him. So he can reassure the populace there that they are being taken care of."

"You really think he can pull that off so easily?" Alex asked. "Tell you what. If he does, I'll throw my lot in with you, but I don't want to hear another word about this till then." He slapped a few bills on the table, stood, and walked away. Victoria didn't say another word but he could feel her eyes on his back as he made his way back to the dormitory.

Chapter 6

Victoria woke Alex with another call the next morning. "You wanted to know when we secured our VIP," she explained triumphantly. "Harris finalized everything this morning."

Alex couldn't believe what he was hearing. In one night, the ambassador had managed what he had thought impossible. Did the research center depend on the support of Eden colony that much?

"You didn't think we could pull it off," she accused, "but we decided on the girl. She seems to have... taken an interest in you. So, anyway, we thought you might be able to talk her into going along with this."

"And if she refuses?" Alex asked, still skeptical.

"She won't," Victoria promised. "They've been trained from birth to follow orders, they're pretty docile. You're pretty fortunate to have been spared all that. We won't be leaving for a few more days. Take that time to prepare yourself. I'll go over everything in more detail before then.

"Oh, and Alex," she paused. "Welcome to the team. I look forward to working together again."

Then she hung up. Alex slumped back in the bed, trying to determine exactly when his world had fallen apart around him.

# # #

Subject 148 sat staring at the ceiling of her room as if she could see through the white expanse. In her quarters, she was able to go without the helmet, which was otherwise ever-present. Her deep, brown eyes were uncovered, and she always marveled at the difference between this and the "other sight" she was forced to employ most of the time.

It would happen soon. She was certain of it. Even before the doctors had informed her that she would be leaving the facility for a short while, she had been sure of it. She was leaving and she wouldn't be back. The doctors didn't know that, and she saw no reason to tell them. They most likely would not believe her anyway.

She found her thoughts turning to the boy again. She still didn't understand. He was like her and the others, but he was freely able to come and go. Why? When she had tried to ask him about it, he had denied it and claimed he had no idea what she was talking about. Still, she was sure of it. She wondered if she would see him again once she left this place. She wasn't sure, but it felt like she would be taken somewhere far away. She wasn't frightened by this, she simply knew it was so.

The longhaired girl she had encountered before, on a rare excursion outside the complex, and again when the young man had visited. She had something to do with 148's upcoming departure, but that was as much as 148 knew. 148 continued to sit silently, pondering her future, until the doctors arrived to run the next series of tests. She rose without complaint, and allowed them to cover her eyes once again.

As she stood, her other eyes opened. Seeing this way was so different from using her physical eyes. This way most everything was visible entirely in black and white. The only exceptions were living things. The scientists and security agents around her stood out from the background in a variety of bright colors. Dr. Mercer always seemed to display a reddish hue, which varied in intensity from day to day. Other people crossed the spectrum, from yellow, to blue, to purple. Interestingly, all of the others here like her invariably glowed a brilliant green, and they had assured her she did so as well. That was why she had been so sure that he was one of them. Somehow, he didn't seem to know that. The doors to the test chamber ahead slid open and she stepped inside.

# # #

Alex was actually glad to return to duty the next day. Regardless of Commander Prescott's opinion on the matter, Alex and the others were cadets no longer. There was little choice in the matter, anyway. The casualties of the previous battle had left gaping holes in the combat roster that had to be filled. Now, he was running a routine patrol along with George. Unfortunately, such a simple task wasn't enough to occupy him completely. His mind raced, preoccupied with everything that had happened in such a short period of time. George had picked up on it, and asked, but he was considerate enough not to press further when Alex had assured him that everything was fine. Obviously it wasn't. "Fine" might be completely out of reach at this point. They reached their next checkpoint, and Alex maneuvered his fighter to head toward the next one. For once, he would not have minded a little action, anything to take his mind off things for even a little while. The kilometers ticked away steadily and he settled back into his seat, watching them drain like the sands of an hourglass.

# # #

Subject 148 looked up as a pair of security officers opened the door to her room. Unprompted, she rose from the bed where she had been sitting, and moved to the door. Wordlessly, they escorted her to the elevator. It was time, she knew. She was leaving, and not just for one of the short excursions they rarely took her on. This time she was not sure if she would ever return. There was a small flicker of fear at the thought, but she reassured herself. If the doctors were sending her out, she would surely be all right. They had always done everything possible to keep her and the others safe from harm, and she trusted them now as much as ever.

# # #

"So, what's the deal?" George grilled Alex as they sat down to lunch. "You've been hanging around with Victoria an awful lot lately." George took a big bite of the steak he'd sprung for. It was expensive, but occasionally they splurged a bit. "What's going on between you two?" he asked between bites.

"Nothing's going on." Alex replied defensively. He had no intention of explaining all of this to George. Best friend or not, Alex had no way of knowing how he'd react. He tried to brush off the question. "She needed some help with some task for her dad, so she twisted my arm. You know how she is."

George snorted at that, but didn't seem entirely convinced. "You never seemed keen on helping her before." He paused and glanced at Alex suspiciously. He lowered his voice, "You haven't fallen for her have you?"

Alex nearly spat out his water at the remark. Coughing and sputtering he protested, "Are you crazy? No way, not in a million years!" He glared angrily at George, indignant that he had even suggested it.

George, meanwhile, had nearly fallen out of his seat laughing at Alex's reaction. "Hey man," he managed to say, "I was just making sure. I'm glad to see you haven't gone crazy on me." They continued to make small talk as they finished their meals.

After lunch, they parted ways. Alex had resolved that today he would finally do what he had been putting off since his time in the hospital. He was headed home to visit his parents. If Victoria really managed to drag him along on her crazy mission, he might not see them again for some time. Taking a deep breath, he made his way out of the military ward toward the residential district.

He passed through familiar neighborhoods, streets he'd known since he was a child. The house he had grown up in appeared before him, unremarkable among the nearly uniform buildings that lined the street. Only the numbered plaque alongside the door differentiated it from dozens of others. That plaque symbolized home.

He paused on the doorstep, still torn over the decision to come here. After a few moments, he hesitantly raised his hand and rung the bell, announcing his presence. A moment later, the door opened to reveal his mother standing inside. Her eyes lit in surprise. She hadn't expected him, as he had not called ahead. He had left himself the option to change his mind at any time. She recovered from her surprise and stepped back to let him in.

She ushered him into the living room. "Would you like anything to drink? Perhaps a snack?" She offered as he took a seat on the couch. "I could make some—"

"It's alright," Alex assured her. "I just ate." She acknowledged his reply with a nod, and then stepped out to call his father in, informing him of the surprise visit. A few minutes later, they both entered the room and took seats across from him. Uncomfortable silence reigned for several tense moments as they sat together in an undeniably tense atmosphere.

Finally, Alex broke the silence. "I want to know," he said. "What you mentioned in the hospital. I want to know all of it." He stared across at them, meeting their eyes. They were visibly uncomfortable, but his father nodded and clasped his hands together beneath his chin, gathering his thoughts.

"When you were born," his father began, "It was the happiest day of our lives." His mother nodded her assent to the declaration, but still could not meet Alex's eyes.

"We were caught up in the joy at the birth of our first child," his father continued. "When they ran the test, and it came back positive, we were devastated. The thought that we might lose you was unbearable.

"We were good friends with the officer who performed the test. I called in every favor I had, and offered him a large sum of money if he would just look the other way. At first he refused, but we begged and pleaded with him. Finally, he agreed. Your records were cleared and we never heard anything about it after that." His father leaned forward.

"We had heard things about that place that made our skin crawl. We just couldn't stand the thought of you being locked away there forever." He laughed suddenly. "If we hadn't succeeded with that, I was planning on stealing a ship and running." The absurdity of the claim was too much. Alex couldn't help but chuckle at the thought.

What he had been dreading and expecting to be an unpleasant visit ended up as a warm welcoming time with family. He realized he had really needed this. Even so, he did not mention to them the schemes he had become caught up in. The only result of that would be to bring them undue worry. He truly didn't want that. In the end, he was glad that he could part with them now on good terms. As he made his way back to the barracks, it felt as if a weight had been lifted from his shoulders.

Chapter 7

Alex arrived at the Eden embassy slightly early. Victoria had woken him yet again, informing him to meet her here. Their gifted candidate had been delivered to the embassy, and she wanted a chance to go over everything, and to instruct the girl on the role she would be playing. *Are we really doing this?* he had to ask himself again. All three colonies were tenuously holding on as it was, and a power play like this was surely more likely to risk that than it was to benefit anyone, wasn't it? Were either Victoria or the ambassador thinking about anything but their own gain? He made his way to the gate and announced himself. A moment later, he was passing through, and crossing to the embassy itself. Unlike most of Nifelheim, the Eden embassy was vividly colored and decorated with bold greens and rich browns to bring to mind the lush and verdant tropical world that was Eden. The Eden flag hung from the pole out front: a bold green expanse, with a yellow circle centered on it. A blue lambda shape cut the circle into three sections, in the same way that Eden's capital was divided by the New Tigris River.

Alex entered the embassy building and was directed to take a seat in the foyer. Victoria had apparently not arrived yet. He waited restlessly, still unsure as to why he was necessary at all to this whole scheme. So far, he had merely been an observer, accompanying Victoria wherever she wanted to go, but surely she had something else in mind, some reason for asking him to be a part of this. Whatever it was, he couldn't fathom it. The rich and powerful apparently moved in ways incomprehensible to ordinary people like him. Ordinary? He'd forgotten that word didn't apply to him anymore either, he smiled bitterly at the irony. Several minutes passed as he sat musing. Finally, Victoria entered through the sliding glass doors. She spoke with the secretary stationed at the front desk, then took a seat next to Alex. In a few moments, the ambassador opened the door leading into the rest of the building and invited them inside.

# # #

Ambassador Harris led Victoria and Alex to a small conference room with a solid wooden table and comfortable chairs arranged around it. Victoria and Alex entered the room and made themselves comfortable while Ambassador Harris ordered an aide to arrange for refreshments, and to bring the gifted girl to them. The aide scurried off to obey, and the ambassador walked into the room and took the chair at the head of the table.

"So then," he began, "your father has indeed given his support, and the council's blessing to my efforts?" He looked to Victoria expectantly.

"That is why I am here," she assured him. "Of course, he can't be here personally, in order to maintain deniability should you fail. Likewise, there will not be a public show of support until you succeed." Of course, she had actually said nothing to her father at all. This was her opportunity and she was determined to reap the benefits, however the cover story was almost certainly the result if she had.

"Naturally," the ambassador snorted. "They'll leave me to take the fall if I fail while expecting to reap the rewards if I succeed. As long as they don't interfere while the coup is underway I'll be satisfied." He nodded his head in satisfaction.

Fool, Victoria thought, *they would have stayed out of it regardless.* Getting involved would put them at risk of backing the wrong party, which could turn out disastrous. Ymir depended on Eden's agriculture to feed the thousands of colonists living here. In the same way, they both depended on rich volcanic Adar for its rich industry and abundance of metals. Ymir in turn, supplied water to fiery Adar, and its abundance of rare elements necessary for electronics and many other applications to both of the other colonies. Disrupting this cycle would be foolish. *Yet here we are, planning to do just that,* she thought, *but the gains here far exceed the risks.*

There was a knock at the door. Then, it opened and a pair of embassy personnel brought in a spread of various Eden delicacies and beverages for them to partake of. Once the workers had cleared out, the ambassador bid them to help themselves to the bounty. There was an abundance of fruits, of course, delivered that day from Eden's fields. Meats from their various livestock, raised in fields too large to be setup on either of the other colonies, were amply provided as well. Beef, pork, and fish from specially bred animals adapted to life far from their planet of origin. Once they were satisfied, the servants quietly cleared away their dishes and withdrew once more.

A few minutes later, there came another rap at the door, and the girl was led in. The security officers directed her to a seat, which she took, and then withdrew to stand just outside. Once they had left, the ambassador began, "Well, the first order of business it would seem, is to decide just what to call you. Subject 148 somehow doesn't just roll off the tongue." He sat considering the matter, rubbing his chin.

"I believe I can help in that regard," Victoria spoke up. "According to our records, her birth name was Sophia Elias. It's as good a name as any, don't you think?" A frown creased the ambassador's face at her revelation, which showed that the real purpose of her revelation had been successful. *That's right,* she thought, *We can pull information freely from your databases.* She wasn't too concerned about tipping her hand. It pointed out rather clearly that the ambassador was dealing with powerful people, and that he should not forget that fact.

"Very well," he agreed, still frowning, "that is satisfactory, and it serves to tie her more strongly to Eden. So be it." He turned toward the girl, seated at the far end of the table, "Do you understand? From now on you will be known as, and answer to the name Sophia." He seemingly had no clear grasp on how aware the test subjects were, or how intelligent they might be.

"Understood," she acknowledged, "this one will be known as Sophia now." She answered in monotone, and with the bulky helmet covering her head it was impossible to determine her expression. Whether or not she approved of the name, she gave no sign. Victoria felt slightly uncomfortable in the presence of someone who seemed balanced squarely between human and not human.

# # #

The meeting moved forward, with Victoria and Ambassador Harris hashing out details, and tackling various contingencies, refining their plans to perfection. Whenever they addressed Sophia, she responded with a direct answer, never expanding upon it, and never volunteering anything. Seemingly, she was as intelligent as anyone else present, perhaps more so, however life as the psychic research center obviously yielded a much different individual than life in the colonies.

Throughout the long hours of planning, Alex caught himself stealing glances at Sophia. He couldn't help himself. Every time he looked her way, she immediately turned to meet his gaze. Invariably, he would turn quickly away. It wasn't so much her, he told himself, as it was a curiosity that this is what he would be if not for his parents' intervention. It was unnerving. Finally the coconspirators reached a satisfactory point to conclude the day's work, and he was able to leave. He parted with Victoria outside the embassy with just a curt goodbye and plodded off toward the barracks.

# # #

It was late when Victoria arrived home, so of course her father demanded to know where she had been, and what she had been doing. She hesitated for just a moment, and then spun together a workable half-truth. She told him about her conversation with the ambassador at the party, stating that the ambassador was interested in some mutually beneficial business arrangements, and that he was interested in speaking with her father in particular.

"If he wants to do business with me, why not approach me directly?" Her father wanted to know, his eyes narrowed. "Why all this sneaking about, meeting with my daughter"

She assured him that it was a matter of the ambassador lacking the confidence to approach him with his ideas, and fears that he would be turned down. Therefore, he had petitioned her to champion the cause on his behalf. Why, she had just met with him at the embassy to hear his proposal and had returned to bring her father a favorable report. He had bought it.

"He knew to come to me, eh?" he muttered, "Obviously a smart man. Probably could work something out..." He turned back to her, "Good work my dear, you'll make a fine politician someday." He turned back away dismissing her as he considered how to best turn this to his benefit.

Sooner than you think father, she promised herself quietly as she hurried away. She needed to speak to the ambassador quickly, before her father did, and ruined everything. She'd throw him a line about her father pretending to contact him with above board proposals in case someone got suspicious. He'd play along, she was sure, and the two of them would talk past each other long enough for her to pull this off. How simple it was to manipulate them. *Should it be this easy?* It didn't matter, as long as she got what she wanted. Nothing else was of consequence.

# # #

Alex had a hard time sleeping that night. He lay awake in his bunk. Tomorrow was it. In less than twenty-four hours, they would leave behind the only home he'd ever known and set out across the vast expanse of space toward an unknown world.

There was little choice in the matter. It was either that or face being exposed and locked away underground for the rest of his life. Some choice. He rolled over again in his bed, futilely yearning for blissful obliviousness that would not come.

Chapter 8

The preparations had finally been completed, and everything was in order. Victoria stood in the hangar bay, alongside Alex, Sophia, and Ambassador Harris. Officially, they were seeing him off on her father's behalf. He had met with the ambassador at length without incident. Neither of them were any the wiser as to her plans. The last of the ambassador's belongings were being loaded, and he was preparing to board. "Ambassador," she turned to him, "might I have one last word with you?" she glanced meaningfully toward the ship's crew milling about.

He caught her intent and replied, "Certainly, come with me, we'll use the ship's lounge. She followed him into the shuttle, with Alex and Sophia in tow. He motioned for them to be seated around the circular table and then asked, "Now then, what is it that you need?" He eyed her, looking curious and slightly nervous at the implications of a need for private conversation so close to his departure.

"I am having some reservations as to whether you can truly accomplish all of this," she began. "It seems rather farfetched for a man like you to accomplish so daunting a mission." The ambassador was beginning to turn red at this sudden attack on his character. This was a big reversal from the way she had treated him before, and he was not taking it well. She got to the point. "Honestly you just aren't the man for this job."

A pair of the ambassador's security officers entered the lounge at that moment. Ambassador Harris turned to them, livid, and barked, "Throw these ingrates off my ship immediately!" The guards stepped forward and drew their weapons, leveling them at the ambassador. "What is the meaning of this?" he shrieked.

"Your staff seems to share my assessment of your abilities," Victoria explained, rising from her seat. "They agreed completely when I told them I'd have a far greater chance of accomplishing this task, and they will be rewarded well for their service." She crossed her arms and regarded the pitiful man, shaking in rage and fear before her.

"You can't do this to me!" he yelled, "I'm a powerful man! I can crush you into dust! How dare you try to double cross me!" He stabbed his finger out toward her in condemnation, his face twisted in anger.

"Those are very bold words," she answered coolly, "for a dead man." His face melted into sheer terror as the guards responded to her statement by leveling their guns at him and firing once. The ambassador slumped, dead, to the floor of the ship. Victoria turned to the guards, "We'll have to keep the body here on the ship at least until we reach Eden. Hide it somewhere it won't be found." With a curt nod, the guards moved over to the body and hauled it away. Alex was staring at her, his mouth hanging open, frozen in shock. Sophia had not reacted at all throughout the encounter.

"Why?" Alex finally spoke in a whisper, "why?" His face was pale, and his hands were shaking slightly. Watching the ambassador's death had obviously affected him more than the sterile, impersonal loss of allies had in their skirmish in space.

"He was in the way," she explained to him, cooly. "We have a much better chance of success without him." She was confident that he'd be able to accept the necessity of this in time. There would be many more bodies before this was over. He would have to get used to it.

"So you just killed him?" he asked incredulously, "He didn't deserve to die for that!" He wasn't getting it. Fine, she would have to lay it out for him, make him see the big picture.

"There wasn't any other option," she told him patiently. "If he'd stayed in charge, we would probably have failed, and if we had left him behind, or locked him up there would be a chance of him tipping our hand, or reporting us. That is a risk we can't afford to take. He had to go." She turned to Sophia, "How about you, do you agree with my decision?" she asked.

Sophia turned her head to face Victoria. "Your analysis is accurate; we have a greater chance of realizing our goals this way. Eliminating the ambassador was a sound decision." There, all the confirmation he needed. She really had weighed all her options. Unfortunately for the ambassador, this was the most practical solution.

Alex had turned his horrified gaze to Sophia now, dismayed at being the minority opinion here. It was too late to back out now. In a moment, the crew would be finished loading her bags and supplies and they would be launching. They had to depart quickly before they were missed. She turned and began making her way to the cockpit to confirm their status with the pilot. She could feel Alex's eyes on her back until the automatic door hissed shut behind her.

# # #

Marcus Barrett looked up as one of his aides approached him, "Sir, the ambassador's shuttle has just launched," the man reported.

"Excellent," Marcus replied. His talks last night with Harris looked as if they would reap significant returns, for Ymir colony, and of course for himself. With this and the surge of support after he oversaw the ceremony for the troops, reelection was guaranteed; he may not even need to pay for a campaign at all. "Inform me at once if he tries to contact me," the aide turned to leave, "Oh," Marcus continued, "Please send for my daughter. I need to speak with her." She deserved a little praise for setting up this opportunity for him.

# # #

Alex lay on his bed. The spacious shuttle was more like a luxury yacht and had enough private rooms for all the passengers and crew. The ambassador certainly hadn't spared any expense on the craft.

Alex could not stop thinking about what had happened in the lounge. He had retreated here as soon as he could, unable to bear being in that place where a man had died before his eyes. He could understand and accept someone killing in self-defense, or even in anger, but Victoria had been completely calm and collected when she sentenced the ambassador to death. She didn't even blink as he was shot mere feet in front of her. Resolution washed over him. He couldn't be a part of this. No matter what Victoria claimed, the ends did not justify the means. He sat up, finally, and exited his room, charged with newfound purpose.

# # #

George looked up as a security officer approached him. He was in the cafeteria grabbing lunch after running a morning patrol.

"Pilots Morris and Barrett have not checked in today, and they missed their assigned patrols," the officer began, without preamble. "Have you seen either of them today?"

"I room with Alex," George explained. "He left early this morning to go somewhere; I don't know where. He's been meeting up with Victoria a lot lately, though. They're probably together, wherever they are." The officer thanked him and withdrew. It wasn't like either of them to shirk duty, but especially not Victoria. George shook his head. Something strange was going on, and it probably wasn't good. He hurried to finish his meal, determined to find his friend and get to the bottom of whatever was going on.

# # #

Alex hesitated at the door in front of him. Tentatively, he reached out his hand and knocked quietly. A moment later, the door slid aside, the room's occupant not saying a word. She sat on the bed inside, looking toward him expectantly. He took a breath, then stepped inside, the door closing behind him. He took a moment to compose himself. He was nervous around her. She sat quietly, waiting for him to speak. This was the smallest of the ship's cabins. It was just large enough to house the bed and a small wooden desk and chair. All three were fastened securely to the deck, like the rest of the ship's furniture. He took a seat on the chair and swiveled to face Sophia.

"Um," he began, "is there any way you could take that thing off?" He gestured toward her ever-present metal helmet. "It's hard to talk to you with it on."

She reached up and began unfastening the bulky accessory. After finally disconnecting various cables and loosening straps, she lifted the helmet free and set it next to her on the bed. He saw her face for the first time. She had brown hair, extending only to chin level. Her skin was ghostly pale, and her eyes were brown and innocent. After a moment he caught himself staring, and forced himself to move on to the purpose of his visit.

"You were right," he admitted to her. "I am like you. I didn't want to admit it to myself, but it's true." Now that he'd started, everything came tumbling out. "But my parents hid me from the research center, and I grew up normally."

For the first time, she spoke unprompted. "Why would they do that?" she asked, looking quite startled. "The center exists to help us. Everything they do is for our benefit." She seemed confused by the seemingly contradictory assertion he'd made.

"They didn't believe that, and I'm inclined to think they're right. I grew up just fine without all the doctors and tests they put you through. I've never worn some metal helmet to keep me under control, and nothing bad has ever happened. You really only have their word that this is for your sake." He didn't know how she would take all this, and now that he'd said it he expected she would probably reject it outright.

She was staring at him intensely. "I don't know what to think," she said softly. "I know that you lived separately from us, and I believe you when you say you experienced no trouble in doing so. But I have never had reason to question the doctors' commitment to us. They take good care of us."

"But you've been confined in one building all your life, you never knew your parents, you're forced to undergo tests and wear bulky equipment! How can you stand all of that?" Wasn't she disturbed by any of that? Did it truly not bother her to live that way? He couldn't understand it.

"I have lived like this my whole life," she said in a voice scarcely above a whisper. "I do not know anything else. This is the longest I have ever been outside the facility." She dropped her head and curled her legs up, with her chin resting on her knees. "I would like some time to think over all of this by myself," she said at last.

"Uh, ok..." he took her meaning after a moment, "I guess I can come back later?" he asked, but she made no reply, already lost in thought. He quietly made his way to the door and slid out. He honestly had no idea if that had gone well or not. He turned and made his way back to his room. It would be several hours before they reached Eden. Might as well rest up before then.

# # #

"When was the last time you saw her?" George had managed to find Liz and Claire and was asking them about Victoria. So far he hadn't been able to find any clue as to her and Alex's whereabouts, and he was growing more concerned.

"I haven't seen her all day." Claire informed him. "We talked to her briefly last night, but she said she had some pressing business her father needed her to take care of." That didn't really jive with the fact that security was looking for them. If Alex and Victoria were on a legitimate errand, surely military command would have known about it.

"Okay," George said, "if you do see her or Alex, let 'em know I was looking for them."

Claire's face flashed concern and she asked, "Is there something wrong? You would tell us if there was wouldn't you?"

"Of course," George lied. "Don't worry about it. I just wanted to ask them something." He turned to continue his search, waving a farewell as he walked off. *Where the hell are you Alex?* he thought to himself. *You'd better be alright wherever you are.*

# # #

"What do you mean you can't find her?" Marcus slammed his fist into the desk. "First I get a report she shirked her military duties, and now you tell me she has somehow disappeared?!" He saw through a mirror across the room that he was turning a rather disturbing shade of red. The aide standing before him was shaking badly. "Get out!" Marcus barked in disgust. The aide scurried away. This was exactly what Marcus didn't need at this point: more stress. He promised himself he'd get to the bottom of this quickly. After taking a moment to compose himself, he picked up the phone and began making calls.

# # #

The emerald orb of Eden grew ever larger in the ship's front view-screen. Victoria stood in the back of the shuttle's cockpit, contemplating her goal floating in the black sea before her. She resisted the impulse to stretch out her hand in front of her and close it around the moon. It was an uncharacteristically childish impulse and she squelched it easily. She turned away with only a hint of reluctance. She had preparations to make before they arrived, and they would be there very soon.

Victoria knew mostly what to expect. There would be high humidity, lots of green, and a generally more temperate environment than in the cold dome of Nifelheim. The people were blindly devoted to their religion, which allowed the leaders to keep order. Whether those in power believed what they preached, she could not say, though Harris seemed to believe they did. Most of the colonies' food supplies grew in the lush climate of Eden without which Ymir and Adar would likely be unable to survive, their own greenhouses insufficient for the task. Victoria took a seat. They would be landing soon.

# # #

Alex felt restless as they stood at the ship's exit door, and tried to keep from fidgeting. Victoria had produced Eden-style clothing to replace Sophia's outfit, which screamed: "research test subject!" She had also allowed Sophia to forgo wearing the heavy, restrictive helmet, and Alex was glad for that. He still felt uncomfortable just seeing it. Victoria and Alex remained in Ymir military dress uniforms, which they had worn to see the ambassador off. Victoria insisted this would make them look more official, and intimidating, to whoever greeted them. A pair of the ambassador's security personnel stood silently behind the three teenagers, their weapons prominently displayed at their hips. This was the first time Alex had ever been on another world, and under different circumstances he would likely be excited.

The door before them began to open with a hiss. The earthy scent of lush vegetation wafted in. It reminded him of his one trip to the large greenhouse back on Ymir, however this was far richer and more vibrant than even that. The guards pushed past them to exit first. After determining that there was no danger, they allowed Victoria to debark. Alex started to follow her. The heat and wetness of the tropical moon struck him as he stepped out, and he began to sweat almost immediately.

# # #

Victoria strode away from the ship purposefully and met the administrator coming toward them. "Where is the ambassador?" He asked, looking curiously at her and the other two young people emerging from the shuttle with Ambassador Harris' guards.

"The ambassador was unfortunately delayed," Victoria informed him, with her best air of authority. "His negotiations with the Ymir council are consuming his time. However he wanted to send the gifted one back to his superiors as soon as possible. Her name is Sophia Elias, and Ensign Morris and I are her official escort."

He bought it. "Of course, Miss Barrett," he replied.

So, he recognizes me... That begged the question of whether he knew her by reputation, or if the ambassador had told others here that he had been working with her. The former was preferable.

"Please, right this way," the administrator continued. "Accommodations will be prepared for you. Take the day to rest from your travel, and I will arrange a meeting with the priests for tomorrow." He gestured for them to follow.

The spaceport they had landed at was artificial-looking by necessity, but the majority of the colony was designed to have a natural look. Wooden exteriors covered modern construction materials giving the city an organic feel. The crystal-clear water of the New Tigris River, which ran through the city, glistened in the sunlight. After a few minutes of walking they reached the building they would be staying in, which was within the city's residential district.

The three-story structure was also covered in a wooden exterior, polished and stained a pleasant dark shade. The second and third stories had glass doors instead of windows, each opening onto a small balcony, allowing occupants easy access to the outside. Eden citizens all seemed to love the outdoors. Victoria expected they would not be very comfortable staying beneath the great dome of Ymir colony. In the same way, she imagined there were some on Ymir who would be unnerved by the vast openness of Eden. Personally, she didn't care one way or another. She was equally comfortable in both colonies. That was a good thing, as she was planning on spending a great deal of time here.

The administrator showed them to their rooms, and then took his leave, no doubt to make a report to his superiors. The accommodations were adequate, she decided—not quite measuring up to the standards she was accustomed to, but suitable for the time being. She would take the opportunity to rest and prepare. Tomorrow, the real game would begin.

# # #

Alex stood on the balcony outside his second-floor room, caught up in the first real sunset he had ever seen. Gold and red light filled the sky, stretching out from the horizon in a glorious display. Beneath the dome of Ymir, he had never seen anything like this. He was enraptured by the sight before him, and almost did not hear the faint knock at his door. He crossed the room to the door, unsure of who might be there. Victoria would not be so hesitant. She might not bother with knocking at all, so who was this?

He opened the door, and was quite surprised to find Sophia standing there. She didn't say anything, but just gazed up at him, looking surprisingly vulnerable. He stepped aside to let her in, and then closed the door behind her. She crossed the room, and took a seat in a comfortable chair set at the ornate wooden table across from the room's bed. He took a seat on the bed and waited for what she had to say.

She began softly, he had to listen closely to hear her, "This is the longest I've ever been outside of the center," she told him. "Something is wrong, my heart is beating quickly, and it's hard to breathe... I've never spent the night anywhere else... I didn't want to be alone... Do you know what's wrong with me?" It all came out in a rush. She looked at him imploringly, a single tear rolled down her cheek, and she jumped at the sensation. Her hand went to her cheek as if this was something she had never experienced before. Given her past circumstances, perhaps she hadn't.

Alex knew exactly what she was feeling. "You're just scared, and nervous." He assured her. "You're a long way from home in an unfamiliar setting. It's really normal." He felt a wave of sympathy and compassion for her. But for his parents' intervention, he would be just like her right now. He stood and walked over to her, taking her hand in his. She looked up at him, worry etched into her face. "It will be alright," he told her. "I won't let anything happen to you." He gave her a reassuring smile.

After a moment, she nodded, and some of the tension drained from her face. She made no move to extricate her hand, and asked tentatively. "Can I stay here, just for a little while?" She was like a child in many ways, innocent, struggling to deal with feelings and sensations that were new to her. He couldn't help feeling protective of her.

"Of course," he told her, giving her another smile. They sat quietly as the minutes ticked away. The last rays of sunlight slowly faded away, until the room was bathed only in twilight. Finally, she pulled her hand away, reluctantly, and stood. She turned and headed to the door to return to her quarters.

At the door, she paused and turned her head to whisper back, "Thank you." Then she slipped out the door, and closed it behind her. Alex sat in the darkness, now more certain than ever that the Psionic Research Center did not have their best interests at heart. To have produced someone so stunted emotionally that she couldn't even recognize her own feelings... Just what did they do to their young wards that left them like this? It would be quite some time before he would be able to sleep.

Chapter 9

The brilliant rays of the morning sun pierced the thin veil of curtains to illuminate the room. Victoria was already up. She had chosen a flowing green robe similar to those of Eden's priests, albeit with a tan sash as opposed to their gold ones. If she was going to appeal to the beliefs and superstition of the populace, she had to look the part. She left her hair down. Simplicity was favored here over extravagance.

She was fully aware that she would need to beat the religious leaders here at their own game, but she was not overly concerned. For one, she had become quite adept at politics from observing her father; secondly, she had something they didn't. Sophia, the gifted girl, would serve as an excellent rallying point. Tying the gifted so strongly into their cult would work against the priests here. Even better, Victoria could have Sophia perform "miracles" at any time to bolster support. Satisfied with her appearance, she turned and headed out to find a light breakfast before starting her campaign.

# # #

Once they had finished a breakfast of fresh fruits and pastries, they were ready to set out. Victoria had cautioned Sophia not to speak unless she prompted her, and to follow her instructions. Sophia had merely replied, "Understood." To Alex, there was no sign of the turmoil and emotions of the previous night. She was back to the submissive, almost unresponsive girl he had first met.

Victoria had broached the subject of some medication the center had left to the ambassador for Sophia to take. Alex had convinced her not to administer it, at least for the time being. His argument was that it could be a suppressant for her abilities and Victoria needed her to be able to wow the crowd. Victoria had bought it, or at least agreed not to use the drugs. Really, Alex simply did not trust the center, or anything associated with it.

# # #

They proceeded toward the main temple complex located directly in the center of the city, where the bisecting New Tigris River forked on its way to the sea. Simple stone or dirt roads lent a quaint, rustic air to this section of the city. A pair of the late ambassador's security officers escorted them down winding streets far less rigid in layout than those of Nifelheim. The temple itself loomed on the horizon. Designed to inspire awe in the populace, the massive building was sculpted out of stone, and towered over the rest of the city. Steep stone steps led upward to the temple proper, and the living quarters for the colony's religious leaders.

They began their ascent toward the summit, and climbing the steps was a feat of endurance in itself. Victoria expected they had been implemented not only to raise the temple above the rest of the city, but also to force a grueling ordeal on anyone seeking to meet with the priests. She was determined not to give them the satisfaction of seeing her winded. She was athletic enough to make good on that promise. Indeed, she found she had to stop and wait for the rest of her party to catch up.

She used that time to drink in the details of the extravagant place of worship. Elaborate patterns, columns and sculptures framed the great staircase. The magnificent opulence was clearly meant to inspire awe, but to one such as

Victoria, coming from a practical culture with value placed in function over form, it was almost laughable. As they finally crested the top, she could see a wide stone courtyard stretching out before them. The temple lay ahead with other facilities bracing it on either side.

It looked as if it had been lifted whole from humanity's distant past. Great white columns supported a massive stone roof. They were met by a servant and led to one of the side buildings where the priests would be meeting them. The man explained apologetically that the temple itself was restricted to believers, and therefore they would not be able to enter.

The man led them to a small room with a simple wooden table and chairs, and asked them to wait while their presence was announced. Victoria seated herself at one end of the table, with Alex and Sophie on either side of her. Her security officers took up position standing a short distance behind her. They did not have to wait long before two men in flowing, green robes entered the room and took up position at the other end of the table.

"I am Brother Benjamin," the elder of the two began. He was seated opposite Victoria and was obviously the senior of the two due to his more ornate robes. "We were concerned to hear that our ambassador was not with you when you arrived, however we understand his business with the Ymir Council was important and he was unable to leave. The question, to put it bluntly, is who *you* are, and why you're here."

"Of course," Victoria smiled graciously. Brother Benjamin already knew who she was. Victoria was sure of it. His bluff had not worked. "I am Victoria Barrett, daughter of Councilman Marcus Barrett of Ymir. As the release of a gifted test subject is a highly unorthodox request, I'm sure you can understand that they wanted an important representative to accompany her to ensure her stay here goes smoothly. I volunteered for the position. I had hoped to visit Eden colony, ideally to return a favorable report to help further strengthen the relationship between our colonies."

The priest nodded slowly. "Admirable," he replied. "You are welcome to accompany the gifted one throughout her stay here, and we look forward to sharing the rich culture and heritage of our world with you." Here he lifted the goblet before him, which servants had brought in while they talked. "To a stronger bond between our peoples."

Victoria echoed the toast, then drank. A light and sweet liquid—juice from one of the many fruit trees growing here—trickled down her throat. Alex and Sophia mirrored her. After a few minutes more of polite conversation, the priests made their exit. They were satisfied with her explanation for the time being, but haste was still necessary. It was only a matter of time before they grew suspicious of the lack of reports from the ambassador, or until they made contact with Ymir to find there were no diplomatic talks occurring. If she was going to succeed here she was going to need another collaborator. Fortunately, Ambassador Harris had already made preparations to that effect and had a list in his personal files of likely individuals. Time for her to go to work.

# # #

It was still difficult for Alex to believe how little he had actually known Victoria. He had thought that, back what seemed like years ago during cadet training, he had her figured out. Now he could see just how wrong he had been. The cold-blooded murder of Harris, and now as she manipulated these priests, always working to further her own ends. She was so adept, like it was natural. Once again, he had to wonder what purpose she had in mind for *him* in all of this.

Victoria had informed him that she had business to attend to here in the temple complex. She had instructed him to escort Sophia back to their residence and stay put for the day. Tomorrow there would be a tour of the city, and the next day Sophia would be brought before the assembled priests. Today they had to themselves.

They reached their lodging and Alex reluctantly headed inside. He was interested in exploring the city but would have to wait for tomorrow to do that. Sophia quietly followed him upstairs, but instead of returning to her room, she followed him to his. Assuming she wanted to talk again, he held the door open for her, and she wordlessly walked in and sat.

He took a seat on the bed and waited for her to speak. "I wanted to show you something," she began. "It's something we learned at the center. The doctors don't know about it, we figured it out on our own." She looked up at him, waiting for his approval before proceeding.

He had to admit he was intrigued. "Okay," he told her, "go ahead." She closed her eyes and relaxed her posture in the chair.

For a moment nothing happened, then her voice rang out clearly, but not within the room, it was in his mind. *"Alex,"* it said simply. It startled him, and he gasped audibly. Sophia opened her eyes and sat up once more across from him. "We used this to talk when we were in our rooms." she explained. "We never felt lonely this way. You can do it too. Then we can talk even when we're alone."

What do I need to do? he instantly wanted to know. Part of this was another test to reconfirm for himself that he did indeed have these strange abilities, and part of it was, of course, that he wanted to be able to talk more with her.

"It's easier if you close your eyes," she told him, "at least at first. Picture the person you want to talk to in your mind, and focus on them. Oh, it only works on people like us though, normal people can't do it. Then, think what you want to say."

It was difficult for him at first, he had never consciously used his abilities before now, but after some time working at it, he managed to call out to her. Opening his eyes, he saw Sophia actually smiling at him, the first time he had seen her do so. His heart beat quickly for some reason upon seeing this, though he didn't know why.

They agreed to end the session there for the day, but she assured him they would continue to work on it when they could. He was sure she was doing this for her own sake as much as his. Going from having dozens of people she could reach out to at any time to total silence must be disconcerting. Evening was falling on Eden colony, and he resolved to get some rest before the long day they had ahead of them tomorrow.

Chapter 10

The next morning, the group ate a quick breakfast, and then headed out into the city. Brother Benjamin had assigned a guide to lead them, and answer any questions they may have. They began in the residential district where they were staying. Their guide made sure to highlight the high standard of living afforded to all citizens, which Victoria noted was certainly far easier to accomplish here in a hospitable environment than on the extreme worlds of Ymir and Adar where so much of their resources were taken up maintaining a livable habitat. Even so, it was clear that the common people of Eden lived well, if not nearly as well as the priests ruling them from on high.

Their next destination was the commercial district. They were making their way counterclockwise around the city's circular layout. Here, the veneer of primitive life was peeled back somewhat. Stores maintained the simple, wooden look on their exterior, but their insides were far more familiar. The goods for sale looked mostly the same as those found at home. Advertisements flashed, and salespeople beckoned. At the same time, there were also some vendors who had taken to setting up small stalls along the road, offering simpler wares and foodstuffs. It was an interesting mix of new and old, unique among the three colonies.

The final district of the city was the military ward. They would not be getting a full tour, obviously, but their guide seemed eager to boast about Eden's defensive force, and their success rate in repelling attacks. This last sector made no pretense at appearing natural or simple. Raw technology and progress glistened nakedly everywhere they looked. The only concession made was a high wall surrounding the entire district, keeping it out of sight from any other part of the city.

The Eden colony *Seraph*-class fighters the group was shown differed slightly from their own *Valkyries*. The *Valkyrie* maintained a balance between armor, speed, and firepower. These fighters, while built from the same base, were designed as interceptors. Speed was emphasized, and their armor was significantly lighter. They relied on that speed and maneuverability for defense, as they certainly would not stand up to many hits.

Regardless of Victoria's, and surely Alex's, thoughts on the matter—being pilots they were not so keen on the increased vulnerability—she had to concede that Eden's continued existence lent weight to the *Seraph* design being a viable option. After meeting a few of the officers in command and exchanging pleasantries, they headed toward the last destination of the tour, Eden's impressive agricultural fields. Their guide assured them that they would be given a tour of the temple complex at a later date, as it would require a full day to cover on its own.

# # #

Alex was immediately struck by the vastness of the open fields stretching almost to the horizon. They had now exited the city through one of its gates, and reached the fields stretching out in every direction from the city itself. The sheer variety of plants grown here was mindboggling. Eden cultivated not only staple food crops, but also trees for lumber, medicinal plants, as well as herbs and spices. The greenhouse back on Ymir he had once thought so impressive was a joke compared to all of this. Their guide seemed pleased by their reactions, and was happy to rattle off all number of facts and statistics to demonstrate the importance of Eden's agricultural efforts.

As they made their way back, the sun working its way down toward the horizon, Alex could only plod along silently, still in awe of what he had seen. It seemed so unjust that the people here had so much, when others on Ymir and Adar were struggling to survive. If those other two moons did not have resources that were sorely needed, it would have been so much better for everyone to concentrate here on Eden. Defending one location would surely be better than three, would it not?

They reached their building and he wearily trudged to his room and flopped onto his bed. He had intended to simply go straight to sleep, not even caring about food, when a voice suddenly, timidly, entered his mind. *"Alex?"*

He bolted upright, startled into full alertness. He took a moment to calm down, then focused intently and managed to reply, *"Sophia?"*

He felt relief in her... voice? He supposed the term worked well enough for this kind of contact. *"I'm just... a little overwhelmed by everything today,"* she admitted. There was a world of difference between her speech and behavior now compared to when he had first met her. He had to wonder again if the drugs the center had wanted her to take and the bulky restrictive helmet played a factor in that. *"It's kind of scary out there, no walls or ceiling. It's so big..."*

He could understand her sentiments. Having lived under the comforting closeness of Ymir's dome all his life, he felt a little nervous in Eden's expansive openness. Having lived in an underground lab for almost her entire life, she must being experiencing the difference even more acutely. *"I know what you mean,"* he tried to reassure her. *"It isn't quite as bad for me since I'm a pilot. Being out in space can be even more overwhelming. Are you ok now?"*

"Yes... I'm alright." After a moment of pause, as if she were hesitating, *"Alex?"*

"Yes?" he thought back to her. This was becoming easier for him the more they practiced it. With a bit of work,

they would be able to communicate in public without anyone knowing.

"What is it like to have parents?" The innocent curiosity in the question saddened him greatly. He couldn't imagine having grown up without his parents, despite the friction he had recently had with them. He took a moment to collect his thoughts and then began to tell her everything he could think of about his parents. She listened intently throughout, enraptured by his words.

Chapter 11

The aide approached Councilman Barrett's desk as if he was nearing an angry bear. The staff were all aware of his temperament over the past few days, and were justifiably wary.

"Sir?" the man ventured, almost flinching as Marcus leveled his gaze at him. "The technicians have gone through the security footage as you requested. This is the last record we have of the people in question." The aide placed the handheld unit with the data onto the desk and beat a hasty retreat.

Marcus took the unit and activated the video. His eyes narrowed as he watched the footage before tossing the unit back onto the desk. He leaned back in his seat and considered the footage. His daughter's last known whereabouts, the hangar bay at the time when the Eden ambassador had departed. The group had entered the shuttle, and had not exited before it departed. There was no evidence to suggest they had not gone willingly, so then why had she not told him about any of this. None of it added up. The difficulty now lay in finding out just what was going on, without letting anyone else know about the problem. He had to maintain an image of being in control no matter the reality of the situation.

Well, he had just the solution in this case. He did have agents already in place on Eden. He'd had a different purpose in mind when they had been planted there, but that was immaterial now. This situation took priority. He picked up his phone and began setting up the process of delivering orders to his covert operatives. It was a slower course of action than he liked, but essential to protecting his agents. Ideally, they would have their assignments in a few days' time. Now he could only wait, and hope for a positive report.

# # #

"It's been three days now!" George exclaimed, slamming his hands on the cafeteria table in front of him. Liz, seated across the table, jumped at the impact, and several people at nearby tables turned to stare.

"If there was a problem, they would have said something," Paul replied levelly. He continued to glare at George until he reluctantly took his seat. "You already said yourself that they took your statement. If they need anything else, they will come to us." George understood what he was saying, he just couldn't accept it. There was something about this that prevented him from dropping it. Maybe it was just the fact that Alex hadn't said anything to him before he and Victoria disappeared.

"Um," Liz spoke up hesitantly, "actually, I did get through to Victoria's dad this morning. He assured me that they were ok. It seems like they're working on something for him and there was just some miscommunication about it." She must have been concerned if she approached Councilman Barrett about it. It was completely out of character for the normally timid girl.

"You see?" Paul interjected, "It's just like I said. Relax; I'm sure they're fine."

Reluctantly, George had to admit that if there was a problem, Victoria's father would certainly be demanding explanations and creating a media frenzy over it. If he said everything was fine, it probably was. He still wished Alex had said something to him before disappearing like that, but the fact that he had been with Victoria a lot prior to this added weight to this story. "Alright," he conceded. "I guess that makes sense. I still won't be completely satisfied until I see them again, though."

#

Alex couldn't help being nervous as he ate. Today, the high priest of Eden would be meeting with them, to speak with and examine Sophia. She didn't seem intimidated by this, but he figured that was mostly a matter of her not completely understanding the significance and magnitude of the situation. He tried to clamp down on his anxiety, not wanting to accidentally transmit it to her somehow. He didn't know whether that was possible or not, but he didn't want to chance it.

For the second time, they made their way to the temple complex. They knew what they were in for this time, and the climb wasn't quite as exerting as it had been before. They were led to another of the side buildings for their audience, this one more elaborate than the relatively humble structure where their last audience had taken place. Once again, their guide reminded them that only believers were allowed in the temple itself, with the exception of Sophia. As a gifted one, she was free to enter if she wished. Victoria endeavored to make it perfectly clear that Sophia would not be going anywhere without them accompanying her, and for the first time since they had boarded the shuttle to come here Alex felt himself in full agreement with her. With that, their guide bowed and withdrew, to report their arrival to his superiors.

As they waited, Victoria reminded him and Sophia how the meeting would go down. They were not to speak unless directly spoken to, and were to stick strictly to the story she had laid out for them in previous meetings. She would handle most of the talking, they just had to keep cool and follow her lead. Alex still felt way out of his league here, meeting the religious leaders of an entire world. Knowing they would take even greater interest in him if they knew his secret did not help matters.

The layout of this chamber was completely different from the last. The three of them were seated together behind a small table on one side of the room. On the other side of the room, an ornate, hand-carved wooden chair was set amidst tiered rows of wooden benches. The priests obviously would take these seats with the high priest taking the throne-like chair. The walls were smooth, white stone, and a red carpet covered the floor in contrast to the simple wood or stone floors of most Eden buildings.

After only a few minutes, the interior door of the chamber opened, and green-robed figures began filing in. The high priest led the procession, his advanced age, and the abundance of gold designs covering his robes denoted his position. With just a hint of exertion, he took his seat. The other priests took positions around him according to rank. Those closest to him being the most senior, with the initiates furthest away.

For some time after they had settled, no one spoke. The high priest stared intently at Sophia, scrutinizing her. She met his gaze unflinchingly. To Alex, she looked every bit as she had when he had first encountered her. Any internal turmoil she might have could not be discerned by looking at her now. Finally, the high priest nodded slowly, as if satisfied by what he saw.

His gaze softened somewhat. "Come forward child." He spoke in a kind, almost fatherly voice. Sophia looked to Victoria, and when she nodded her approval, slowly stood and moved to stand in the center of the chamber. "Sophia," he said. "Taken from us fifteen years ago. Yes, there is no mistaking it. Welcome home child." Sophia made no reply, simply meeting his gaze.

# # #

The high priest turned to address Victoria. "I must confess that we were surprised by your willingness to allow this visit. Relations with Ymir have always been... somewhat strained. Your preoccupation with the sciences has left you, shall we say, disinclined to tolerate our beliefs." There were some murmurings among the gathered priests around him at that.

Victoria smiled indulgently in the face of the critique. "I'm sure that there is certainly some weight to that, but such idealism has waned significantly on Ymir in recent years. The war continues to drag on, chipping away at the resolution of many. Honestly, I myself had ulterior motives for coming. The unwavering faith of your people intrigued me, and I hope to learn more about your faith while I am here."

There was dead silence from the other side of the room at her admission, and Victoria briefly wondered if she had over played her hand. She needn't have worried. The next moment, applause broke out, and the high priest gave her a warm smile.

"It is heartening to see such open-mindedness in the young. In truth, we had long since abandoned hope of being able to reach the people of the other colonies, but you have rekindled that spark. Please, feel free to speak with any of the priests here during your stay. Ask your questions. We would be delighted to share our faith with you."

The meeting wore on for a while after, but formality had been abandoned for a friendly atmosphere. Instead of increasing suspicion, Victoria's gamble had worked almost too well. The priests wanted so desperately to expand their sphere of influence that they had fallen all too easily to the bait. Now, she had an alibi to spend much more time at the temple complex, and to meet with the contacts she was engaging, those on the ambassador's list. This had been a most fruitful meeting for her indeed.

# # #

The meeting had finally concluded after Victoria had prompted Sophia to demonstrate some of her abilities for the duly impressed priests. She had made sure to emphasize the research center's role in refining both ability and control for the subjects. Now as they made their way back down the massive steps, Alex wondered how much truth there was to the claim. He understood her reasons for making it, but the truth of it was irrelevant to that. The real question was that if the center was not working to those ends, what ends was it working toward? That was what troubled him. He was likely over thinking things, but for some reason he simply couldn't let go of this. Deep in thought, he continued the descent to the city below.

# # #

Silent, silvery shapes streaked through the void undetected. Large, ovoid ships filled with tightly packed forms, braced by the sleek, deadly slivers of interceptors. This was one of three clusters launched simultaneously toward the three, fragile orbs making their ponderous journey around the bots' planet, captives of its pull. The ships' occupants did not discriminate between, nor even appreciate the differences of belief that the inhabitants of these worlds felt so keenly. The humans were all indistinguishable to the machines, and they all needed to be eliminated. The fleet of vessels pressed on, slowly drawing closer to the verdant green sphere hanging before it.

# # #

Alex woke to the sharp rap of someone knocking on his room's wooden door. Groggily, he got up and made his way across the darkened room to open it. Victoria stood outside, "Hurry and get dressed," she said. "There's an attack wave incoming. They want us to observe."

Fatigue vanished instantly at that. The colony was under attack. He hastily threw on his clothes, then hurried out to follow her. Alex went to wake Sophia as they moved downstairs to where their guide was waiting for them. He led them out and down the vacant streets toward the military district.

Something was bothering Alex, but it took him a few moments to realize what it was. There were no alarms blaring. Eden was under attack, but it was deathly quiet. Either the leadership was very confident in their ability to repel assaults, or they were forsaking the safety of their people in order to maintain an artificial air of peace and tranquility.

They passed through the gate into the base, and the difference was immediately evident. This was more what he expected during an emergency. Everywhere, uniformed personnel were moving with haste and purpose, preparing to repel the assault. Their guide directed them to one of the command buildings nearby. Once inside, they were cautioned to remain in the back of the room and quietly observe.

Tactical screens covered the walls, and a holographic field projected from above hung in the middle of the room, with officers huddled around it. The swarm of red blips displayed there was sizable, but not the largest Alex and Victoria had seen. That prize went to their first and thus far only real engagement.

# # #

High above the Ymir colony, *Valkyrie* fighters streaked across the vacuum of space, eager to tear into these unwelcome intruders. Angry, red light lanced toward them from well beyond their firing range, but this time they expected it. Formations held and pilots stayed calm, patiently waiting for the distance to close.

George weaved his way through the firestorm, watching the kilometers tick away. His targeting reticule pulsed gold as he closed into effective range. Lining up his target, he clamped down on the trigger finally able to retaliate. Ruby energy scored the side of the drop ship leaving welts in its hull. The larger ship tried to turn away and escape, but it was slow and ponderous compared with the agile fighter. George stayed on it, pumping more shots into it until it burst apart in a fiery detonation. He turned away, seeking another target.

They were making quick work of the attacking force he noted, once again raising the question of why the AI had always sent such small fleets in the first place. He couldn't dwell on that now, especially since the last attack had proven so effective. He set his sights on an interceptor that had just torn apart a *Valkyrie*, delivering vengeance in two bursts that sheared the silvery craft in half. Most of the larger vessels had already been destroyed. The remainder of the fight would just be mop up. He sought out another target.

#

Regardless of her opinion of the Eden leadership as a whole, Victoria had to admit that their military, at least, was in competent hands. The senior officers directing the battle demonstrated great skill and ability as they directed the course of the battle being waged overhead. Squadrons of *Seraph* interceptors cut through the attacking fleet surgically and efficiently. Casualties were surprisingly low considering the craft's light armor, and the engagement was in the process of wrapping up now, far faster than she had expected.

This was both promising and potentially dangerous for her. It was clear now that it would be necessary for her to cultivate alliances here as well as in the temple complex if she was to succeed. This attack, and their subsequent invitation to observe, had been most fortuitous for her in that regard. If these competent individuals remained stubbornly loyal to the fools on their pinnacle, it would be quite problematic. She would have to proceed carefully.

Chapter 12

The light of sunrise roused Alex the next morning despite the late night excursion. Victoria had informed him on their way back that she would be out today on her own, with instructions for him to stay put here with Sophia. Unfortunately for her, he was disinclined to follow those instructions. He had decided he needed to get out and take another trip through the city. He was still fascinated by the culture of this place, so foreign from what he was used to. He was also looking forward to taking his time without a guide dragging him around. He made his way to Sophia's room, and knocked on her door softly, not knowing if she was up yet. A moment later, she answered the door.

"Uh, hey," he greeted her, "I was thinking of going out and taking a walk around town. Would you like to come along?"

"We were told to stay here," she reminded him. She was used to following orders, having done so all her life, but Alex made an effort to persuade her nonetheless.

"Yes," he admitted, "but I really don't feel like staying cooped up in here all day. There's so much I want to see and do while I'm here. You were born here you know." Her head jerked up at that, and her eyes bored into his. Apparently, she hadn't known. "Don't you want to experience the world you came from?"

That did it. He had her interest now. She warred briefly with her inclination to do as she was told, but her curiosity won out. "Okay," she said softly, "let's go." He smiled encouragingly and led her down and out of the building into the bustling streets of Eden. The contrast from last night was immediately apparent. The streets that had felt wide and empty of life then, now were bursting with life, filled with all manner of people pressing toward their destinations. The two of them drew no attention as they slid into the crowd. Without their guide, marked in the robes of a temple official, they looked just like anyone else.

They worked their way off the bustling main road onto quieter side streets where they could take the time to drink in their surroundings. Alex reveled in the crisp fresh air, so different from the recycled air of the dome. In the relative privacy they had, even Sophia let herself relax somewhat. She would occasionally smile as Alex pointed out different things as they walked, infected by his eagerness. More and more she was opening up to him, losing the impersonal feel of the lab, maintaining it only in the presence of others.

They discovered a small park in the residential district, an open, grassy area with a few trees and flowerbeds in place. This was more fascinating to him than even the vast fields outside the city. This was the closest he'd ever come to an actual natural environment. They drank it all in, exploring every inch of the park before stopping to sit and rest beneath one of the trees.

Alex was gasping and sweating from exertion, but he felt better than he had since arriving on Eden. The world was so filled with life, he felt himself full of energy like never before. He had never imagined a place like this could even exist. Sophia sat next to him, quiet but happy, smiling softly.

"You were right," she admitted quietly. "I'm glad we went out. Thank you." She turned to face him. "I've experienced so much since I left the center, it's overwhelming some times. But the one thing I'm sure of is that I'm grateful I got this chance. I don't regret a moment of it."

"I'm glad to hear that," he told her. "I was actually really reluctant to go along with all this, to come here and all, but I feel the same. I'm glad I got this chance now. I don't regret any of it either." He meant it, too. His whole outlook had been irrevocably altered. The sheltered perspective of a boy living under a sheltering dome had been shattered first in his trial by fire, and now by this glimpse of the greater universe. He couldn't go back to that now, but that was fine.

He was startled when she actually laughed softly at his declaration. He was becoming used to her smile, but he had never heard her laugh until now. Misunderstanding his startled expression, she apologized, "I'm sorry, you just always seemed sure of yourself to me, so it was strange to hear something like that."

"It's ok," he reassured her, "I just hadn't heard you laugh before—" he stopped there as she turned away, reddening slightly. He kicked himself for it. Suddenly, she jumped up and started running. "Hey!" he called after her, but she didn't stop. He tried to keep up with her, but lost sight of her as she slipped back into the busy streets. Great, he'd really done it now. Victoria was going to kill him. Frantically, he dove into the bustling streets to search for her.

#

Victoria bid the priests she had been conversing with farewell as she left the small building. There were more individuals dissatisfied with their position here in the temple complex than one would think at first glance, and her new contacts here had also been helpful in naming several promising candidates for collaborators among the senior military staff. It seemed all was not perfect here in paradise as the leadership wanted them to believe.

The difficulty still lay with time. Things were progressing, it was true, but at this rate they would be ready to move in a few months instead of weeks as she needed. She needed some kind of rallying point to attract supporters with. That meant using Sophia. It was a bit early to bring her trump card into play, but she didn't have much choice in the matter. She could either gamble big here and risk losing everything, or wait and lose it all anyway when the web of deception she had woven around them came apart around her.

It wasn't difficult to set things in motion, suggesting a ceremony where the high priest could present Sophia to the masses had been met with great enthusiasm. Apparently, they had considered the idea, but they had been reluctant to approach her about it. They had expected reluctance from Ymir's representative over a formal religious event such as this. She made sure to remind them of her conversation with the high priest, reaffirming a more open-minded culture than they feared. It was still a blatant lie, but they embraced it eagerly as truth. The more Victoria played this game, the easier it became, and all the more intoxicating at that. It was distancing her from Alex, she knew, but she also knew he would come around once her efforts bore fruit. He would realize that she'd done what she had to do for the sake of everyone.

Preparations had begun at once for the event, scheduled two days from now. At the same time, they would announce their latest victory over the AI aggressors of which the populace was still blissfully ignorant, and make a large celebration out of it. She honestly couldn't have asked for a better setup than this. For now, she needed to focus on spinning this as best she could to advance her goals. Indeed, if she hadn't been sending forged reports from the Eden Embassy on Ymir to the priests on the ambassador's progress, she would have been uncovered by now.

# # #

"You what?" Victoria yelled incredulously at him when he broke the news to her. He had searched fruitlessly for Sophia for hours before finally returning to their rooms hoping she had come back. Instead he had run into Victoria returning from the temple complex. It was evening now, and the failing light would hamper a search.

"Do I need to remind you how important she is to our success here?" she railed at him. *You mean 'your' success,* he thought to himself, but he didn't dare vocalize it. Of course he was also worried, but that was because he cared about Sophia as a person, not as a commodity. Regardless, they were on the same page. They needed to find her as soon as possible.

Victoria was already speaking with her security personnel trying to organize a search effort. She refused to contact the priests at this point, as she would look incompetent if they learned she had lost track of her charge. It was a tricky situation for her to be in, and he could feel her ire over it. Surprisingly, she didn't seem to be directing it his way as he would have expected. The guards sprinted off to carry out her orders.

Alex tried to discretely reach out to Sophia using the techniques she had taught him. Try as he might, there was no answer, nor any sign of her. Whether this was due to the distance between them, or her intentionally avoiding him, he could not be sure. He made one more attempt before giving up.

"What are you doing just standing there?" Victoria asked him, irked by his apparent idleness. "You're the one who got us in this mess, get out there and find her!"

Victoria looked more flustered than angry, but when he started to protest the futility of randomly running around such a large city looking for someone, her glare cut him off. Sighing, he turned and stepped outside once more. He had no idea where to search, and he was starving. He hadn't eaten in hours, and hadn't gotten a chance to grab anything before being sent out again. Aimlessly, he wandered the now quiet streets of Eden alert for any sign of Sophia, but not truly expecting to run into her. He wondered if she was all right, out here on her own. Thinking about her alone and afraid somewhere spurred him to put more effort into his search.

He ran through the broad tranquil lanes of the commercial district, its stalls closed down for the night. Some shops were still open at this hour, and he poked his head into these just in case. No luck. He pressed on, combing the streets as best he could. He reached the gates of the military district and turned back. Here at least was a section he could skip. There was little chance she had slipped past the alert guards.

The temple complex was also unlikely. She would be recognized there, and he didn't think she would feel comfortable alone among the priests who revered her. He turned back to the residential district to give it another sweep. If he didn't find her there, he would have to stop for the night. He was tired and hungry, he couldn't keep this up. He would have to hope she had found somewhere to stay for the night.

Maybe she had returned to their rooms while he had been out. He plodded back to check on that possibility. When he arrived, he found only a still brooding Victoria waiting for him. She was clearly still frustrated by the unresolved situation, but he was too exhausted to care. Soon, however, she left and he was able to eat before returning to his room and collapsing into his bed.

Chapter 13

The next day, Victoria sent him out again to find Sophia. She was busy with meetings up at the temple complex, and canceling them would draw unwanted attention to their situation. That was how he found himself tasked with searching the entire city alone to find the missing girl. *Wonderful,* he thought to himself.

Several hours passed fruitlessly. He combed the residential and commercial districts thoroughly without success. The bustling crowd made for slow progress. He had just made up his mind to try the temple pavilion when he thought to try contacting her again. Without much hope for success, he found a quiet side street free of the crowd, and reached out to her. He was startled when he almost immediately felt a response.

She guided him to a small residence nearby. There were no words exchanged, they were communicating on a deeper level. When he reached the front of the building, she stepped out from inside. A woman followed her out, explaining that she had found Sophia last night wandering the street and had invited the poor lost girl in.

Alex thanked her profusely for her hospitality before leading Sophia away. They didn't speak as they made their way back to their quarters. An awkward silence still reigned. He sincerely hoped he hadn't permanently ruined his chances of getting to know her better. They reached the building and stepped in to wait for Victoria.

# # #

"Package delivered. Report expected within forty eight hours," the simple message proclaimed from the datapad in Marcus' hand. There was no sender listed, nor anything else to tie it to the espionage agency which answered to him. If they claimed they would have results for him in forty eight hours, then he would indeed have them in that time frame. These were the best of the best, handpicked. If anyone could get to the bottom of whatever was happening on Eden colony, it was them. He would just have to be patient until then, a tall order for him. His blood pressure had been up again over the past few days, exacerbated by this crisis. *Just a bit longer now,* he reassured himself. *We'll get to the heart of the matter.*

Elections were coming up again soon, not that he was worried. Still, he sometimes envied the governments of Eden and Adar who didn't have to worry about such things. He could never admit such things to his constituents of course, but even so it would be far easier to run the colony without worrying about things like public image and approval ratings. He sighed in the privacy of his office, maybe he was just getting too old for all of this.

# # #

Sophia sat in her room contemplating the day's events. She was glad she had taken Alex's invitation and defied her orders. It was the first time she had ever done so. Thinking about him reminded her of the moment in the park and her heart began racing again though she didn't understand why. A conflicting torrent of emotions, all new to her, flowed through her. She dropped onto her bed and laid there letting the sensations wash over her until she fell asleep.

#

That night, Victoria laid out her plans for them. The ceremony sounded innocent enough to Alex, his only concern was how Sophia would hold up to being thrust into the spotlight like this. She didn't seem anxious about it, so he kept quiet. Unfortunately, this would bring an end to any excursions like yesterday's. Once the masses knew who she was, there would be no way to set foot outside unnoticed.

He still hadn't spoken to Sophia since the park. He sincerely hoped he hadn't screwed things up permanently. He really enjoyed spending time with her, the only person he could really talk to on this whole world. Victoria was certainly out of the question. He didn't even know her anymore. His friend and classmate was now replaced by some scheming aristocrat bent on obtaining power. Perhaps this had been the reality all along, and what he knew was only a front.

He resolved to try to talk to Sophia tonight. He really wanted to take tomorrow, the last day open to them now, to spend time with her again. Victoria was still going on about preparations for the ceremony, but that was of no importance to him, and he tuned it out. She would no doubt go over it again tomorrow regardless. He busied himself trying to figure out what to say to Sophia that night, too caught up in his own manageable troubles to be interested in grand schemes far above his head.

That night, Alex tried to contact Sophia while lying in bed. *"Sophia?"* he sent, reaching out to her. There was no response, but he could feel the connection, and knew she could hear him. *"I'm sorry about yesterday. I didn't mean to upset you. I did really enjoy getting to hang out, and if it's ok, I was hoping we could do so again tomorrow."* No response. *"Um, well, sorry again, and if you would like to, just let me know tomorrow, ok?"* He broke off there, unsure of how she felt or what she was thinking. He just hoped he hadn't screwed things up completely.

Chapter 14

Today was the day. Alex shifted nervously in his seat. He was situated to Victoria's right, with Sophia on her left. They had been given seats in the plaza of the temple complex, from which the high priest would address the massive crowd gathered at the base of the great stair leading to the complex. Nearly the entire population of the colony, thousands of people, had gathered. Those performing essential duties would watch a live feed on portable displays. There was an electric air of excitement he had never felt before.

He had not had a chance to talk to Sophia before the event, Victoria had kept the girl close to her, giving instructions and taking her to various meetings. He hoped to get a chance afterward once everything wound back down. The event would begin shortly, and he hoped to put all this behind him.

The crowd of priests and temple workers crowded around the temple itself parted as the high priest stepped out and began making his way across the pavilion. Cheers rang out below as large screens set up for the audience broadcast the starting of the ceremony.

The high priest stopped several meters from the top of the stairs, stepping up to a podium that had been prepared. "My children," he began, "this is indeed a blessed day. Long has it pained us to send away our gifted ones to the laboratories of Ymir, so far from us. It was in the interest of peace that we did so, working with the other worlds so that all may prosper. We had since despaired of seeing any of these blessed ones again. Thanks to the efforts of our ambassador, and some few individuals on Ymir, one of our own has now returned to us." A cheer went up at his proclamation, and he let it die down before continuing.

As he spoke, the high priest continued slowly moving toward the edge of the great stair case, the mass of people gathered at the base pressed against the barricades cheering their leader. He stopped at the edge of the stairs raising his arms. "We are truly blessed," he told them. He explained the battle that had taken place a few days prior. Many craned their heads, staring into the sky as he spoke. He described the encounter as a great victory, further evidence that the Departed Ones still watched over their chosen people. He threw his arms wider still at this pronouncement, and the crowd erupted into cheers, and then shouts of terror and disbelief as he then lost his balance and fell forward.

Stunned silence reigned as temple officials rushed to the still form now lying a third of the way down the staircase. Security personnel immediately began working to disperse the crowd, but they were unwilling to leave with their leader's fate unknown. Alex felt sick in the pit of his stomach. At the high priest's age and judging by the absolute stillness of his body, there was little chance of him surviving a fall like that.

# # #

It was several hours later that they finally made it back to their quarters. Alex was tired beyond belief, and sickened by what he had witnessed. He just wanted to go upstairs, drop into bed, and pass out, until he heard Victoria comment, "Well, that went even better than I expected." His blood froze in his veins. He couldn't comprehend what she was saying at first, then suddenly he knew. It was unbelievable, even for her, but there it was. Somehow he knew it was the truth, and he felt rage building inside him at the very thought of it.

He wheeled back around, glaring at her. "You!" He shouted, "You made her—" he couldn't say it. He turned to look at Sophia and his heart sank when he did. She looked just as she had what felt like eons ago when he had first seen her face on the shuttle. Expressionless eyes met his without even a hint of the life they had shown recently. Had Victoria put her back on the drugs?

His eyes snapped back to Victoria. "You monster! How? Why? He was a good man!" Her eyes widened at that.

"Good?" she replied in an incredulous tone. "He's just like all the rest of them. They're playing these people for fools! Leading them on with lies! Don't pretend he's some innocent old man. I did what I—" her head rocked back violently as his hand connected with her face, leaving an angry, red mark.

The next moment Victoria's security officer knocked him to the floor. His head was throbbing. He had just enough time to look up to see Victoria's face, open-mouthed with disbelief, before the security officer brought the butt of his gun down again on Alex's pounding skull delivering him to merciful oblivion.

# # #

A throbbing headache heralded Alex's return to consciousness. He carefully pushed himself up to a sitting position and took stock of his surroundings. He was on a narrow, wooden bunk in a small, unadorned room. Three of the walls were bare rock. The fourth was thick glass with a security door set into it. He had been thrown into prison, wonderful. He started to regret his actions until he remembered the blank look on Sophia's face. Anger welled up in him again, but he was helpless to do anything now. He turned that anger on himself, now she was alone out there with Victoria, and he was totally unable to help her. He sat on the thin bed for a long time, kicking himself over his rash action. Despair set in, and he curled up on the cot longing for sleep.

Chapter 15

Victoria stood before the majestic temple clad in a simple, white robe. The smooth stone of the pavilion felt cool against her bare feet. The robe's hood was drawn over her head covering her hair. She looked every bit the humble religious convert. Appearances, of course, could be deceiving. There was no penitence in her heart.

She had been anticipating this moment for some time. This was a crucial element to her plans. If she wanted to gain the trust and approval of the people, she would need to appear to convert to their beliefs. The road to this point however, had been a dangerous one. The priests would be naturally skeptical of a person from Ymir, notorious for skepticism and rigid scientific study, suddenly showing an interest in their faith.

She had moved slowly and patiently, starting with basic curiosity. She asked the priests about various aspects of their faith as she met with them. They invariably responded enthusiastically, eager to share their beliefs with her. The more she spoke with them, the more open they were, and she was soon able to express seemingly genuine interest in their faith.

From that point, she had been able to convince her various contacts among the priesthood to support her, and sponsor her request for conversion. With the backing of several influential priests, she had quickly found herself invited to several sessions designed to teach her the doctrines of the faith, and prepare her for conversion.

She paid close attention to these sessions with genuine interest. It was important that she learn as much as possible about the religion of Eden if she was to lead the people in the future. Her teachers were pleased at her enthusiasm and she had progressed quickly.

Today was the day she would finally be accepted as a member of their faith. Her conversion would allow her to enter the temple itself and improve her standing with the people greatly. She was eager to proceed, but did her best to look humbled and subdued for appearance's sake.

Before her, several members of the priesthood flanked either side of the path ahead of her, facing inward. They were resplendent in the green and gold robes of their office. The priest waited inside to perform the actual ceremony. The conversion was a private and sacred ritual so there was no crowd to witness the events. Only Sophia accompanied her, following behind her as a witness. She stood silently now, the silver helmet masking her face.

The sound of trumpets rang out from inside the temple as the ceremony began. Slowly she began to move forward, walking along the path before her. The priests to either side chanted in a strange language as she passed. She honestly wondered if it was a real language at all, or if they had simply made it up.

She reached the steps leading up into the temple itself. Beneath her bare feet, she could feel the rounded edges of the steps, worn down by the masses of believers who gathered here to worship weekly. The great white columns supporting the temple roof loomed ahead. They were like something out of the ancient past from a time when humanity had worshipped the very elements as gods.

It was fitting in her mind, as she saw the beliefs of these people as being every bit as primitive. She passed between the columns, out of the bright light of the sun, into the dim light of the temple interior. A long hallway stretched out before her, with a large room at the end of it. She made her way down the hall moving at a slow even pace to match the solemn atmosphere of the occasion.

She stepped into the great room where the new high priest waited for her. He smiled warmly as she approached. She wondered if he had ever presided over a conversion ritual before. Citizens of Eden were born into their faith, and she couldn't imagine many people traveling from Ymir or Adar as she had. The priests from outside filed in behind her, forming a circle around her, the priest, and Sophia, and the ceremony began.

Solemnly, the new high priest stepped toward her. He stopped a few feet away. She had memorized the ceremony in anticipation, and knew her role well. Smoothly, she dropped to her knees before him, the chill of the stone floor piercing the thin veil of the robe. She ignored the discomfort, focusing on the moment.

The priests surrounding them took up their chant once more. The high priest lifted his arms toward the ceiling as the chanting reached a crescendo, and brought them sharply down as the chanting abruptly ceased. He stepped closer to her, she kept her head bowed, resisting the urge to look up at him.

"Victoria Barrett," he began. "You have come to us as one who was lost, ignorant of the true path left to us by those who came before. You have devoted yourself to the study of the way and come before us now seeking to join with us." He turned his head to sweep the circle of priests surrounding them.

"Can anyone present attest to the veracity of her claim and of her desire to embrace the faith?" One of the priests stepped forward.

"I do." He stated solemnly. After the first, several more priests stepped forward as well, echoing his statement. Her supporters had been true to their word, and voiced their support here and now.

"Victoria Barrett," the high priest continued, "Do you solemnly vow to uphold the tenants of our faith and live in accordance with them now and evermore?"

It was the only vow required for her to be accepted into their religion. She answered easily. "I do." There was no truth in her reply, but it hardly mattered. Many of those present to hear her utter it were already with her, the others did not matter.

The high priest dipped his fingers into a small jar of oil he carried, and spread it across her forehead. "Rise Victoria Barrett," he proclaimed, "child of the departed." A cheer rose up from the assembled priests as she stood. A genuine smile spread across her lips. She had just cleared one of the final obstacles in her path. There was plenty of reason for her to be pleased. Soon everything would come to fruition. She would be able to fix all her problems.

# # #

Alex wasn't sure any more how long he'd been here. The lights of the prison were on at all times, and there were no windows. The room was sound proofed, so he could not even speak with the other inmates. He had tried several times to reach Sophia, with no luck. Either she was too far away, or she was not willing to talk to him. Were they going to keep him here indefinitely, or did they have some other fate in mind? He wasn't sure which would be worse at this point.

He was in the process of leaning back on the bed, when a flash of red light shot past his cell. He bolted back upright. Two security officers in green uniforms moved into view, backing away from something and firing. The leftmost officer was struck in the chest by a blast and fell back, a smoking hole in his chest. The other guard turned to see his partner fall and was shot in the head while distracted, crumpling next to the first.

Another man in an identical uniform ran up to Alex's cell door and swiped a key card across the pad. The door slid open, and the man addressed Alex pointing his gun at him. "You, move." It wasn't a request. Keeping his hands visible, Alex rose and crossed over to the door. The man prodded him in the back with the pistol and they started moving down the hall. Another officer was stationed at the intersection ahead, alert for any movement. When they reached her, she joined them, the three of them moving swiftly. Alex followed their directions without protest. They reached a door and stepped out into the open night air, taking off across the open ground around them toward some foliage ahead. They continued on for several minutes before finally stopping.

The man produced a blindfold, holding it out to Alex, he kept his weapon trained on him with his other hand. Alex took it without a word and put it on. He didn't know what was going on, but it had to beat rotting in a cell for the rest of his life. They continued on for some time after that, his captors directing him as they went. Finally they stepped inside some kind of building, and after several more turns, he was directed to remove his blindfold.

He took stock of his surroundings. He was in what seemed to be a warehouse, several armed individuals stood around him. Crates and boxes of various shapes and sizes filled the cavernous space. One of the men stepped forward and addressed him. "Alex Morris, I am Commander Andrews of the Ymir special forces. We have some questions we need you to answer." Alex's blood ran cold. He'd heard things about the special forces, none of them pleasant. One of the other officers pulled up a chair for him, and he took it, feeling slightly overwhelmed. "Now," the commander began, "why don't you start at the beginning and tell me exactly how and why you're here. Alex took a deep breath, collected his thoughts, and told them what he knew.

He started with the events back on Ymir when he first became aware of things. The commander wanted specifics, names, dates, and times. There was a lot that Alex simply could not tell him. He had no idea how Victoria had first made contact with Ambassador Harris, or why they had started conspiring in the first place. He also was careful to skirt around his reasons for agreeing to help her. The last thing he wanted was for the man to find out what he was.

Every step of the way, he had to clarify points, repeat sections of his account, and provide enough detail for the commander's satisfaction. The man was trying to catch him in a lie, Alex knew, and he had to proceed very carefully, especially since he wasn't providing the whole truth in the first place.

He explained their visit to the research center, and the purpose behind it. The commander seemed particularly unhappy as he detailed the relative ease with which they had secured the release of one of the test subjects into their care. He made several entries on the small computer pad he held at that point.

Next Alex came to their meeting aboard the shuttle and Victoria's sudden betrayal of the ambassador. There was no challenge to this portion of his testimony so it either fit what the commander knew, or he simply didn't feel the need to contest it. He skipped over the uneventful journey to Eden and continued from their arrival. Here the commander nodded as he recounted the events. It was likely that he was aware of these events, hearing from various sources. He seemed amused by Alex's reaction after the death of the high priest, snorting a laugh out as he recounted the slap that landed him in prison. The commander sat back and considered the testimony for a few moments before finally nodding once and standing.

Alex was led to a corner of the building, and ordered into a small office there. Once he was in, they locked the door behind him. They were no doubt discussing the situation and determining what to do, both with him, and the others. He really wasn't any better off now than he had been in the prison. The only thing that had changed was that he knew someone on Ymir knew they were here, probably Victoria's dad, and he'd felt it necessary to send in special forces. He would probably know everything soon enough.

A rap came from the door, interrupting his thoughts. "Just sit tight kid," the commander's gruff voice came from the other side of the door. "Considering how cooperative you were, and the fact that you haven't really committed any offences, other than going AWOL of course, we'll make sure you get off lightly. We'll be back for you after we deal with the others."

"What's going to happen to them?" Alex wanted to know. He wasn't even sure if he cared what happened to Victoria at this point, but he was concerned for Sophia.

"The council will have to decide what to do with Ms. Barrett. Getting to her will be difficult now, since the coup."

Alex couldn't believe what he was hearing, "She actually pulled it off?" *Of course she did,* Alex thought. *This is Victoria we're talking about.*

"Yeah, it's a real mess out there," the commander responded. "Half the priests are dead and most of the population is in a panic, but there's no mistake. At the moment, she's top dog. Anyway, she'll have to go before the council. The gifted girl, one forty something, she'll be returned to the center, of course. Anyway, sit tight. We should be back in a few hours."

Alex heard footsteps moving away from him, he was having a hard time breathing. He had forgotten about that. Of course they would want to take her back there. The thought was unbearable to him somehow. He didn't want her to go back to the lifeless husk he had first encountered there deep below the surface. He wouldn't let them do this. His hands clenched into fists, and he slammed them into the door. The guard posted outside yelled for him to stop, but he ignored the warning. He felt helpless here, the door was too strong.

Suddenly, he knew what he had to do. All this time, he'd had the strength, but he had simply allowed events to sweep him along. Not anymore. He had a purpose now, and he'd do everything in his power to achieve it. He focused all his will on the sturdy metal door before him and *willed it to move.*

In an instant, the solid metal door was torn from its frame and hurtled across the warehouse. One of the agents cried out in surprise. Alex started walking, taking careful measured steps out of the office, and across the warehouse. Agents drew their weapons and leveled them toward him, ordering him to stop. He kept going. A bolt of crimson energy crackled toward him, but it was suddenly stopped a meter from him, harmlessly dissipating. Several more shots met a similar fate. Comprehension was dawning on the faces of some of the agents. One of them reached for her com, trying to issue an alert. The device crumpled inward in her hand, crushed into a broken tangle of electronics. She dropped it with a gasp.

Alex continued moving forward toward the building's exit. No one made a move to stop him now. They stood frozen in place, simply watching as their captive escaped before their eyes. He reached the door, and stepped out into the cool Eden night air. He didn't know where he was, but it didn't matter. He knew where Victoria would be. He located the illuminated spire of the temple on the horizon, and began making his way toward it. He didn't care what happened to this planet. He wasn't even interested in stopping Victoria. To hell with all of them, he decided, but he wouldn't let them use Sophia like this. He would get her out of here no matter what.

The city was dark as he made his way through the streets. It had always been quieter at night, but this was unnatural. There were no signs of life at all, no sound and no people whatsoever. He passed through the residential district without incident. The cloak he had taken from an unoccupied market stall to cover his prison jumpsuit blended him into the shadows. The great staircase to the temple pavilion lay just ahead. Two guards carrying rifles were stationed at the base of the stairs. They caught sight of him as he approached. They leveled their weapons at him and shouted a challenge. He didn't have time to deal with this. He turned his attention to the first guard. Suddenly the man was hurtling through the air to slam into the side of a nearby house, crumpling on impact. His partner gave a yelp of surprise, only to be dispatched the same way a moment later.

The way was clear now. Alex had been surprised how naturally these strange abilities came to him, how effortless they were to use now that he knew how. He didn't relish this power, but he was grateful for it if it could help him accomplish his goals. He began making his way up to the temple complex. Impatiently, he pushed himself to move faster, unsure what to expect when he reached the top.

Finally he drew near. Sweat rolled off of him, and he was breathing heavily from the exertion. There were more guards above, patrolling the area. He did not want to draw more attention to himself, so he moved forward carefully now, keeping to the shadows and slipping between patrols. A pair of guards ran past, making their way to the stairs and then hurrying down them. The guards at the bottom were probably expected to check in at certain intervals. He needed to hurry now. Security was about to get a lot tighter.

He knew exactly where to go. If Victoria had indeed taken over, there was only one place she could be. He carefully made his way toward the temple itself. There were more patrols here, slowing his progress. He saw an opportunity and slipped past a patrol, sprinting as quietly as he could up the steps of the majestic structure. He passed between the massive columns supporting the roof, and slipped into the building itself.

There was gold inlaid in the walls and the floor as well. There was no doubt that this was the most opulent, lavish building in the entire system. The people of Eden had spared absolutely no expense in the creation of their place of worship. At any other time, he could have spent hours admiring the impressive display, but not this night. He made his way deeper into the temple, not entirely sure where he should go.

Finally, he heard voices ahead, and moved forward to investigate. As he drew closer, he recognized one of the voices. His instincts had been right. He pressed closer, peering carefully around the corner ahead. There. Victoria sat at the far end of a large and ornate room. Likely this had been the high priest's audience chamber, and she had taken it over. Several officials and security personnel clustered around, and he spotted a silver-helmeted figure standing along the back wall. Sophia... it hurt to see her like this. His anger threatened to boil up again, but he clamped down on it.

He took a moment to breathe and prepare himself, then he stepped out from his cover and began striding purposefully across the room. He was in plain sight, but he still was able to cross half the distance before he was noticed. Several of the guards turned and leveled their weapons. One of them ordered him to stop, and he complied. The gathered temple workers, and several priests here to suck up to their new ruler, huddled together behind the guards, unsure how to react to this strange figure. Victoria stared at him curiously, but guardedly. The hood of his cloak masked his identity so she did not recognize him.

Slowly and carefully, he reached up to grasp the hood, and pull it back, revealing his face to them. Victoria's eyes went wide with shock, and her face paled. Some of the security officers recognized him, and moved forward cautiously, weapons still fixed on him. The next moment, their guns were smoking useless clumps of metal, sparking in their hands. They dropped the weapons in surprise, and he started forward again.

One of the guards gathered his courage, and ran forward to engage him hand to hand. He made it halfway, before being thrown back suddenly the way he came, hitting the ground hard. A second guard fared no better. Throughout the scuffle, Alex kept striding confidently forward, not slowing at all. None of the other guards made any move to challenge him, and the civilians present gave him a wide berth, scrambling to get out of his way.

He stopped just short of where Victoria sat, meeting her eyes. He stood for a moment, simply staring. She was almost trembling, and her face was as white as a sheet now. He turned to the crowd behind them and said. "I need to talk to your boss for a moment. Alone." There was steel in his voice. This was not a request. They scattered, and scrambled out of the room. Even the security officers retreated. Once they were gone he turned back to Victoria.

"Surprised to see me?" he asked. "You shouldn't be. You were the one who revealed to me the truth about my past. I've just finally come to accept it." She didn't respond. She was up against a wall, and she knew it. "I'm not here for you," he assured her. "If you want to play queen here, then go right ahead. I don't give a damn about that. I'm not even sore about you locking me up. I'm here for one thing." He pointed to where Sophia still stood against the wall to Victoria's left. "Her."

Victoria's eyes narrowed into a scowl, and she finally found her voice. "You fancy her do you? And so you're going to take her for yourself. Don't you dare act like your better than m—" That was as far as she got before the polished wooden throne beneath her shattered into thousands of splinters. She fell backward and landed on the pile, looking up at him with terror etched into her face.

"No," his voice was soft but there was a cold razor edge to it. "I'm nothing like you. I'm taking her out of here so she can have a chance at a real life. What she chooses to do with that is entirely up to her. I just can't stand the thought of her being used by people like *you* anymore." He turned and walked away. Sophia said nothing as he approached. He took her hand in his, it was ice cold. "Let's go," he told her. She offered no resistance, and followed along behind him.

"So that's it then?" he heard Victoria behind him. He paused for a moment. "You're just going to leave?" Her voice had an uncharacteristic quaver to it. "I wanted to share all of this with you, you know." Her voice was tinged with regret. "I did all of this for us—"

"No," he cut her off. "You did it for yourself." She had no answer. Without even a glance back, he started walking again. Sophia followed along behind him obediently. He didn't look at her. It was too painful to see her like this. They exited the great room, and he guided them easily through the halls of the temple. Soon they approached the grand front entrance, the massive columns rising alongside of them.

The pavilion outside seemed abandoned. There was no sign of the patrols that had been making there rounds when he entered. Perhaps they were waiting in ambush ahead. It would make no difference if they were, they were merely an annoyance to him now. Now that they were outside, he did stop and take the time to remove Sophia's helmet. Dull eyes without a hint of the vibrancy they had held only days ago met his. Pained, he dropped the accursed device and continued on, with her trailing a short distance behind.

They reached the bottom of the stairs without incident. The city before them lay empty and lifeless. That suited him just fine. They had to get offworld, and there was only one place they could find a ship. He set out toward the military ward and the spaceport located there.

# # #

Victoria looked up at the sound of footsteps approaching. She wasn't sure how long she had been sitting here, in the ruins of the ornate chair, but she hadn't had the strength to move since she had fallen here. She caught sight of the approaching figures and her eyes went wide. Three Ymir special forces agents moving toward her, unhurried, but with purpose. "Where are they?" he demanded of her. "Where are the gifted?"

"They're gone." She had nothing to gain by lying. "They left some time ago, there was no way I could stop them." She managed to recover some of her composure, and push herself up to stand. "I guess this is it then. You've come to bring me back?" She was caught off guard when the agent laughed in her face.

"You little fool," he bit out. "We don't give a damn about your little power play now. Removing you now could cause this whole colony to fall apart. The instability you caused has pushed it to the breaking point. No, you can keep your little kingdom. Right now the real danger is two bloody gifted running around without any safeguards in place."

Her confusion must have shown on her face, for the officer sighed and shook his head. "You have no idea do you? Let me spell it out for you then. The illustrious research center on Ymir exists to *suppress* the abilities of psychics, *not* enhance them. A rogue like your buddy, who hasn't had any suppression done to him is our worst case scenario. The entire system is in jeopardy now thanks to you."

She listened carefully as he explained everything to her. The purpose of the psychic research center really was to suppress the abilities of gifted individuals. Ideally, the goal was to prepare them for combat application, but that was a secondary goal. He revealed that many scientists had been alarmed by actions taken by gifted individuals during the war with the AI, but the decision to take drastic measures came only after one individual sacrificed himself in a nuclear blast, seemingly willed into existence, so that others could escape during the desperate evacuation from the planet.

The leaders of the colonies had decided that they could not risk allowing any individual to wield that much power, so the center was created to find ways to inhibit these abilities. "That's why this is such a big deal." He concluded. "The girl isn't as big a deal. Even without the drugs and equipment, the center's treatments will keep her from doing any major damage, but the boy; he's a disaster waiting to happen." He pulled out a communicator and tossed it to her. "So you're going to cooperate fully if you don't want your little kingdom here to be a smoldering crater, got it?" She glared icily at him, but took the device as they retreated to give her some privacy. She began making calls as Andrews had demanded, but the content of those calls would be entirely of her choosing.

# # #

Upon reaching the military ward, their progress had slowed considerably. Here at least, there was no mistaking the colony as lifeless and empty. Soldiers were everywhere, and apparently they had orders to subdue Alex at any cost. He had been able to shrug off their attempts thus far, and the Eden colony soldiers' aim was horrible. Shots seemed to bounce everywhere but at him. Still, every encounter took its toll. Although it had seemed effortless at first, using these abilities he had only recently learned to wield did have an effect, and he wasn't sure how much longer he would be able to continue using them. Finally they made it to the hangar bay where the ships were stored.

Unfortunately, the interceptors used by Eden's space forces could only hold one person. He swept the hangar with his eyes, looking desperately for an alternative when he noticed the ambassador's shuttle in a berth near the far wall. *Perfect.* While he had never flown anything other than a fighter, he was confident he'd be able to manage the luxury vessel. They made it across the hangar to the ship without incident.

To his surprise, the hatch was not locked. Apparently they didn't expect anyone to make it across an entire military base to steal a shuttle of all things. He led Sophia aboard, then sealed and locked the hatch behind them. They made their way forward to the cockpit. He made sure she was settled in the copilot's seat before situating himself in the pilot's seat and turning his attention to the controls. Before he had made more than a cursory examination, a squad of soldiers appeared in the hangar entrance. They caught sight of him and opened fire with their side arms. The shots glanced off the ship harmlessly, but drove Alex to greater haste.

Deciding he was confident enough, and running short on time, he started the engines and lifted the craft into position for takeoff. Things were a bit shaky at first as Alex adjusted to the ship's greater mass, but he was soon able to compensate. The only obstacle remaining was the massive hangar door blocking their exit. Alex cursed. If the Eden military had followed standard procedure, the hangar door would be polarized, limiting his weapons' ability to blast through it expediently. Even so, he turned to the ship's defensive weaponry to solve the issue. The troops scattered and fled as bright ruby lances erupted from the shuttle's cannons transforming the door into slag. Alex marveled at these troops' ineptitude. As soon as the way was clear, the shuttle shot through the opening as Alex set the engines to maximum burn. They blasted away from the colony like they had been launched from a cannon.

Eden's greenery shot past beneath them in a blur. Alex pulled back on the flight yoke setting them on a course for orbit. He allowed himself a moment to breathe. The worst of it was over. Somehow he had pulled it off. He still had no real course of action or destination. All of his focus had been on getting this far. He would have to— The ship shuddered violently as if struck. Checking his instruments, Alex was alarmed to see a trio of ships pursuing him, *Seraphs* most likely. He rolled the ship out of the line of fire but it responded sluggishly due to its bulk. They weren't out of this yet.

# # #

"What are those idiots doing up there?" Commander Andrews, the leader of the Ymir Special Forces unit, raved from where he stood next to Victoria in the small operations room in the temple. "They should have easily destroyed that shuttle by now." His frustration was amusing. It showed that in one area at least, she held the upper hand here. She knew the people of this planet far better than he did, and she had their loyalty. If he wanted to get anything done, he would need her help, and he knew it.

"You really don't understand?' she asked, mock surprise in her voice. He wheeled and glared at her, his eyes demanding the explanation he was too proud to ask for. "They know who is aboard that ship," she explained. "The same girl who has been paraded around the colony as their savior. If you think they're going to risk her safety then you're a fool."

"Then you order them to destroy it!" he shouted in exasperation, thrusting the communicator at her. She made no move to take it, keeping her arms folded across her chest.

"Don't be absurd. They would refuse, and it would serve only to weaken my position here. They have orders to try to disable the shuttle so we can retrieve the occupants. That's the best you're going to get." She met his angry gaze with a level cool one, daring him to contradict her. The fighters actually had orders from her only to fake pursuit, but Andrews didn't need to know that.

"Let's just hope," he said at last, "that it will be enough." He turned his attention to the tactical display again. A moment later, one of his operatives informed him that the high priority line he had requested to Ymir had been established. She followed him over to the terminal which provided near instantaneous communication with any other terminal within the same star system.

"Victoria?" her father's flustered visage appeared on the screen with the other council members visible behind him. "What is going on here? Explain yourself young lady." He demanded. Seeing him squirm like this was just priceless to Victoria.

"Hello father," she began drolly. "In case you are not aware, I am in fact the acting regent of Eden colony and I expect to be addressed as such." There was a buzz of astonishment and disbelief from the council members all talking at once. Marcus himself was quite unable to speak for several minutes as he struggled to grasp the implications of that statement. Finally he turned to address Andrews.

"Commander Andrews, what is the meaning of this?" he demanded. "What the devil is going on over there?"

"She is correct sir," the commander reported. "Regent Victoria successfully executed a coup of Eden colony over the course of the last few weeks, using the gifted subject Ambassador Harris petitioned for as a rallying point. The former high priest and most of his supporters died during the takeover. Currently her rule is uncontested." Stunned silence settled over the council in response to the words. The revelation was too ludicrous to believe and yet it was all true. Victoria could barely keep herself from beaming with pride as her accomplishments were laid out.

"I remind the council that there are more pressing issues to deal with currently." The commander continued. "We have an emergency situation with two gifted, one without any inhibition treatment whatsoever, at large." This raised another flurry of commotion among the council members.

"What exactly do you want from us?" one of them spoke up, addressing Commander Andrews. "What is the worst case scenario we're looking at here?" The other council members quieted to hear his response.

"We actually have no idea as to the full potential of a renegade gifted." he replied. "The biggest demonstration of power we have seen is of course the nuclear scale explosion during the AI war, however there is nothing to suggest that this is the limit of their abilities. We have no idea how much damage they could actually do." Dead silence again filled the air in response as this revelation sunk in. "Therefore, I urge you to send any military forces you can spare to engage the target craft and take it down at all costs.

"Due to the nature of their beliefs, the Eden military will only commit to attempting to disable the shuttle. We need that craft destroyed, ladies and gentleman. I am not exaggerating when I say that the fate of every man, woman, and child in this system rests on that." He pounded his fist into his palm to drive home the point.

"I'm afraid I have to disagree with your assessment." Commander Andrews turned to stare incredulously at Victoria as she spoke up. She pressed forward with her point. "If you engage while my forces are up there, you could incite full scale war between our colonies. Were you not paying attention when I said that the people of Eden revere that girl as a messiah? You kill her and you'll have an entire world full of enraged people on your hands, and I will not be able to dissuade them." Some of the council members paled at the thought of that.

"If what Andrews claims is true, we must consider that an acceptable risk." Her father spoke up. "We will cross that bridge when we come to it. This situation is far more dangerous and must be dealt with." The council debated the issue for several minutes before putting it to a hasty vote. Intervention won by a large margin. "So be it," Marcus said. "I want a squadron in the air and on intercept now." Several council aides scrambled to see to it.

"I sincerely hope you do not come to regret this decision," Victoria told them. She turned and moved back toward the tactical display. She had to focus now on capturing that shuttle before the Ymir forces arrived if she wanted to avoid an interplanetary incident. She heard her father's voice calling after her but she paid it no mind. He was no longer of any consequence to her.

# # #

George paled. There were gasps from several of the assembled pilots at the revelation they had just been given. "Could you repeat that sir?" he asked the lieutenant briefing their squadron.

The lieutenant complied. "Target is an Eden diplomatic shuttle. Occupants consist of two rogue gifted, Sophia Elias and Alexander Morris. Elimination of this target is absolute highest priority. Morris is a previously undetected psychic and is considered extremely dangerous. I repeat that the elimination of this target is highest priority. You are to ignore any and all other targets until it is destroyed." He paused for a moment. "I know that many of you knew the target previously during his service here, but I assure you that he represents a very real threat to everyone in this colony. I expect you all to put aside your personal feelings and complete your assignment, am I clear?"

"Yes sir," the gathered pilots responded. George felt crushed. How could this be happening? Alex, a rogue gifted? Was this some sick joke? He had known Alex all his life, he wasn't a threat to anyone. He started to head toward the hangar when the lieutenant called to him, "George Simmons, one moment."

George stopped and turned, letting the other pilots file past him as he looked expectantly to the lieutenant. The man waited until the other pilots were out of earshot before he began. He looked slightly uncomfortable about something, and George could guess what he was going to say before he started.

"Simmons," he began, "We're aware that you were close to the target, and that this might be difficult for you." He hesitated here, "Frankly, command has requested that you sit this one out. They feel it would be a conflict of interest for you out there. It will be hard enough for the other pilots to take out one of their own as it is."

George had been right, and even though he had seen it coming, he was still angry after hearing it. "They think I won't be able to do what I have to, or worse, that I'll help him get away." He accused the lieutenant. "I can assure you sir, if they tell me that Alex is a genuine threat to this colony and the people living here, I will carry out my orders and eliminate that threat. But..." he emphasized the last word, "they had damn well better be right."

The lieutenant didn't respond to that. George's eyes dared him to object to the implied threat, or to insist that he sit the mission out. When no reply came, he slowly nodded and continued on his way to the hangar with a heavy heart. He had meant what he had said, though he had felt sick as he said it. If his friend really was a threat he would have no choice but to carry out his orders.

He climbed the bright yellow ladder to the cockpit of his fighter and settled into it. He was preoccupied as he mechanically ran through his preflight checks, wondering if this would be the day he was forced to kill his best friend.

# # #

The ship shuddered from another near miss. Alex wasn't sure how long he would be able to keep this up. The only reason they had lasted this long was that the *Seraphs* seemed to be intent on taking them alive. That was the only explanation he could come up with. For better or worse, he had been forced onto a course headed back toward Ymir. Another volley swept past his left wing, prompting him to roll the craft right. The shuttle groaned in protest at being forced into a maneuver it wasn't designed for.

Sophia sat passively in the copilot's seat next to him. Thus far she had not reacted at all to the firefight around her, causing him to fear the worst. Would it even be possible for her to return to the way she had been? What had they done to her anyway? He couldn't dwell on any of that now. The console beeped an incoming text message from Eden:

> Ymir fighters incoming. Seraphs will protect you.
> Psychic center is a prison - represses abilities.
> Do not return to Ymir.

Victoria? Alex wondered. It had to be. Still, he pushed her out of his mind. Now unable to return to Ymir, he wheeled the shuttle around and focused completely on getting them through this in one piece. That run towards Ymir almost cost him everything. Brilliant red bolts sizzled mere meters to the right of the cockpit, coming from the front.

A cluster of *Valkyries* loomed dead ahead of him, as the message had warned. He swore, and threw the ship into a dive. There was no mistake here. The Ymir fighters were shooting to kill. It pained him to even consider that the pilots of those fighters were likely friends, brothers and sisters in arms. He maneuvered as best he could, but the shuttle took several hits. They wouldn't last long at this rate.

Suddenly, one of the *Valkyries* erupted in a brilliant explosion, cored by a pair of ruby lances. The *Seraph* interceptors pounced on the newcomers like hornets whose nest had been disturbed. Alex was able to put some distance between them and the skirmish in the ensuing confusion. He wasn't sure exactly what was happening, but he was grateful for it. He tried not to think about whether the pilot of the destroyed fighter had been a friend as he focused on escaping.

# # #

Victoria found herself at the communication terminal once more. "You brought this upon yourselves," she informed the Ymir council members shouting angry threats at her. "I warned you what the consequences of your course of action might be, but you went forward with it anyway."

Her father addressed her, red faced and almost shaking. "We demand that you order your ships to disengage. This is an act of war, Victoria!"

Her eyes narrowed as she crossed her arms over her chest. "I would take care not to make such statements rashly, councilman," she cautioned him. "I understand that you are quite dependent on our agriculture in order to feed your people. You wouldn't want to jeopardize that would you?"

He paled at the thinly veiled threat. The other council members suddenly fell quiet. "You wouldn't dare," he answered shakily. "You're just as dependent on us for several key resources. None of our colonies could survive without the others."

"I can assure you," she replied with a tight-lipped smile, "that you need us far more than we need you. A shortage of equipment can be dealt with for quite some time, but try explaining to your populace that they will have to survive on the meager harvest you can manage from your greenhouses and see how they react." Several of them were visibly squirming at the thought. She had them over a barrel, and they knew it.

# # #

The *Valkyries* had fallen back in disarray, and the *Seraphs* had turned their attention to Alex. It appeared Victoria was willing to help him escape death, but she wanted him and Sophia back in return. The *Seraphs* aimed to disable the shuttle's engines, and Alex could see two military shuttles inbound, armed with grapplers. The problem now was that the only avenue he had for escape was toward Pavonis Prime itself. He had finally resolved that it was their only real chance. The interceptors would be reluctant to pursue him to the surface. The planet represented the very real threat of the AI that now occupied it uncontested. Alex was banking on the belief that they would not be expecting a human vessel to actually land here. At the least, they could lay low long enough to slip away again at a later time.

His suspicions seemed to be accurate. The *Seraphs* peeled away as he drew near the upper atmosphere of the vast sphere of Pavonis Prime. Finally, they turned back completely and abandoned pursuit. Alex breathed a sigh of relief and set a course for atmospheric entry, hoping the presence of one ship might go unnoticed.

# # #

Victoria studied the tactical screen before her. The situation had taken a drastic turn in the past few minutes. After she had given the recall order to the squadron pursuing Alex—they refused to pursue him into the atmosphere so there was no point leaving them out there—several unidentified craft had been detected on long range radar inbound from the planet. Another attack fleet was inbound from the AI.

Commander Andrews had finally withdrawn with his team, after the obligatory threats for her to watch her back. She promised herself that she would devote a team to rooting him out when she had a chance. The thought of executing the arrogant fool brought a smile to her lips. For now, she focused on directing her first space battle as regent of Eden. Proving herself here would help to solidify her grip on the world. Everything else could wait.

# # #

"What?!" Marcus roared at the announcement made by the now terrified aide before him. "Another fleet inbound?" The other council members looked grim and nervous, their nerves already frayed by the day's events. "Recall all our ships immediately! We have to see to our defenses. Get Admiral Anderson on the—" he stopped midsentence as the fluttering sensation in his chest spiked. He had ignored the tightness and then discomfort during the encounters with his daughter and the events after, but this was scaring him. He clutched his chest, gasping with quick, light breaths as he weakly sank to his knees, feeling as if he was about to pass out. Several council members cried out in shock and fright. He felt aides clustering around him and heard someone shouting orders as darkness clouded his vision. His daughter's face flashed in his mind, the cold, defiant expression she had worn when she addressed them earlier, as the regent of her own world. Then everything went dark.

# # #

Relief mixed with the anxiety of the upcoming fight. George still seethed over the casualties they had suffered at the hands of the unexpected Eden attack, but now at least they had a target he could engage with a clear conscience. He'd had Alex's shuttle in his sights several times during the brief engagement, but he had been unable to pull the trigger.

He hadn't trained to kill other people, much less his best friend. Unthinking machines, metal monsters, were one thing. Taking a life was completely different. The familiar sight of enemy vessels filled his forward screen. They were still far out of position from their pursuit and it would take several minutes for them to join the rest of the Ymir forces in battle. He waited impatiently as the distance closed, trying desperately but unsuccessfully, not to think of Alex.

# # #

The surface of Pavonis Prime stretched out before them. It was breathtaking to Alex. Eden had seemed so vast to him, but the scale of a planet dwarfed the worlds he had known. He couldn't help but marvel at the vastness of the world. He had located an area near one of the abandoned cities with no sign of activity, and had decided it was as good a place as any to set down.

If the AI did have any aerial surveillance, the shuttle would look less out of place here than it would in the untouched wilderness. Their approach went unchallenged, and he managed to land the craft without incident. Now, he turned to Sophia and considered her for a moment, finally having a chance to think. She sat staring straight ahead. Finally, she spoke softly, and he had to strain to hear her.

"Why?" she whispered softly, "Why did you come back for me?" Her face maintained a neutral expression, but there was a hint of deeper emotion in her voice. It gave him some hope that he might be able to reach her still.

"Why?" he repeated, "Of course I came back for you, why wouldn't I?" He truly didn't understand her question. What was she talking about?

She turned to face him now, and her face finally cracked into a deeply sorrowful expression, wracked with anguish. "I... I killed them," her voice was softer still. "I did it."

Gently, he reached out and took her hands in his. She flinched and tried to pull away, but he kept hold of them firmly until she finally looked up to meet his eyes. "Sophie," he said gently, "that wasn't your fault." She started to shake her head in disagreement, but he continued on, "You've been conditioned all your life to obey orders, you were drugged, and who knows what else. Victoria killed those men. I won't let anyone else say otherwise, not even you, understand?"

She managed a slow nod after considering it for a long moment. A single tear streaked down her face, and she was startled by the unfamiliar sensation. That first tear broke a dam inside her, and more followed. Alex held her as she sobbed uncontrollably, letting out a lifetime of emotion that had been kept walled up inside her. The two sat quietly in the cockpit sharing their first real moment together in weeks, unaware of the furious battle taking place high above them.

# # #

George cursed as a volley of energy singed his wing. The fighting was more intense now than anything he had ever experienced. This was even worse than that first battle, which seemed like ages ago. He and his squad mates were already taxed by their previous engagement before they had even joined the battle, and that was taking its toll. Casualties had been high.

An interceptor was glued to his tail. The silvery sliver of a ship stuck to him despite his best efforts. Then, a burst of fire suddenly ripped through the craft, vaporizing it. George recognized his rescuer. "Thanks Paul," he called out, "I owe you one." Before Paul had a chance to respond, George watched in horror as a salvo from one of the massive drop ships ripped through his friend's fighter, helpless to prevent it.

There was no chance he had survived. Blinking back tears, George turned on the offending vessel with fury, pouring shot after shot into it until it exploded in a cloud of debris. Someone was calling out to him on the radio, trying to get his attention, but he ignored it, uncontrollable grief and anger surging through him. He tore through the attacking ships recklessly. He lost himself to vengeance struggling in vain to sate the emptiness he felt. The battle raged on around him.

# # #

Victoria tried to process what she had just heard. "Excuse me?" she asked the messenger who had delivered the report. He repeated his report. "Leave me," she ordered, watching to make sure he was gone before dropping to her knees on the floor of the great chamber. Her father was dead. A heart attack, the report claimed. Attempts to revive him had been unsuccessful. A chill swept through her body, and for once she was at a loss for words.

It had only been a few hours since she had exulted in displaying her new status for him to see. It wasn't supposed to end like this. This wasn't fair. She struggled to reign in her churning emotions. She had never wished any harm upon her father; she had merely fought to demonstrate her own merit, to step out from his shadow. Now it was too late. She would never be able to hear him acknowledge how far she had come. She would never hear him say he was proud of her. She felt a tear coursing its way down her cheek and she angrily swiped at it. It was a futile gesture, as it was joined by several more. She allowed herself to mourn the loss she felt so keenly for several minutes unashamedly before she clamped down on herself again. This wasn't the time for this. She would allow herself time to grieve later. Now she had more pressing issues to deal with. With renewed determination, she returned her attention to the battle that continued to rage in orbit.

# # #

Alex surveyed the area outside the ship's hatch, carefully looking for any sign of danger before setting foot on the surface. After a few moments he took a step outside, aware that he was the first person to do so in years. Sophie waited anxiously in the open hatchway. He wasn't sure what exactly had compelled him to use the nickname, but it felt better, less rigid than Sophia, and she hadn't objected to it. Taking another look around, he finally turned and gestured for her to join him. Hesitantly, she stepped out of the ship and walked over to join him.

They stood there a moment, just the two of them, on the surface of an abandoned world. The wind whipped around them somehow adding to the desolate feeling. He turned his attention to the small cluster of buildings nearby. There was a two story central building, with several smaller ones clustered around. Something seemed odd at first, but he couldn't place it, finally he realized that the lights in the building were on. There was still power here. He started moving toward them to investigate further. Sophie followed along behind him. He kept alert, unsure of whether this was evidence of a robot presence, or simply a matter of some ancient generator still running after all these years.

They entered the complex, and there was still no sign of anyone or anything occupying the buildings. He approached the central structure and pressed the button alongside the door. It slid open smoothly releasing a gust of stale air from inside. He carefully surveyed the interior before stepping in. The faint glow of terminals cast a pale light inside, indicating working computers. There was no movement, so he cautiously stepped inside. After Sophie joined him, he sealed the door behind them. Finally, he turned his attention to one of the terminals.

The machine responded to his touch, and an image filled the screen. A figure in a white lab coat stood before him. The figure began to speak, some sort of recording. He and Sophie took a seat in front of the terminal to hear the message.

"March 25, 2183. We have arrived at the site and have begun a preliminary investigation. The mining team has unearthed an object of unknown composition. We have thus far been unable to retrieve a sample of the material, but its properties do not match those of any known material. Further testing is required." The entry ended, and a second began to play.

"April 18, 2183. Today we hope to finally take a sample of the object. Excavation around the initial site has revealed that this is a much larger find than previously expected. We have cleared over 90 square meters thus far, and we have yet to completely unearth the object. Dr. Carter is leading a team down to hopefully extract a portion for further testing, they should be returning shortly." A deep rumbling boom came from somewhere off-screen. "What was that?" the figure asked someone off screen. The recording cut off, but a third followed after.

"April 19, 2183. Rescue efforts to extract Dr. Carter's team from the tunnel collapse yesterday were unsuccessful. They were dead before we could reach them. Work continues slowly now. One of the engineers observed some strange behavior from one of the mining bots today, and is investigating. It's most likely a minor issue and nothing to worry about." The last detail was not lost on Alex and he prayed this wasn't the prelude to what he thought it was.

His fears were confirmed by the next log: "April 20, 2183," the now bloody scientist began with effort, "Something has gone terribly wrong with the AI units at the camp. The engineer who was investigating the issue yesterday was found torn in half near one of the barracks. Soon after, they came for the rest of us. I have barricaded myself here in the central building, but I do not know how long I can hold out. If anyone is receiving this, please send help." The figure whirled around as a heavy pounding noise came from his left. He let out a scream of terror and then the recording ended.

They sat in stunned silence for several minutes. This was it. Some twist of fate had delivered them to the place where the whole mess had started. This was the very camp where the AI revolt had begun. A sudden realization dawned on Alex. The room in the recording had been in disarray, and their narrator had been covered in blood. Looking around now, the room was spotless and sterile. The door, which had been clearly broken down in the log was also fully repaired. The implications sent shivers down his spine. Had the robots cleaned and repaired the facility, and if so, why?

Regardless, the knowledge of the brutal murder that had taken place in this room was too much. He couldn't stay in here any longer. As he led Sophie out, the sun was already touching the horizon. He headed back to the shuttle. They could manage for quite some time on the ample supplies and amenities within. In the meantime, they could decide on their next move.

# # #

Victoria sat in her new spacious quarters, luxurious as was fitting for the regent of a world. Officially, she was titled as the "Great Prophet of Eden," speaking for their saviors the gifted ones. The people had accepted her readily with Sophia providing her with miraculous demonstrations as needed. After the high priest was out of the way, it was a simple matter to play the remaining priests against each other while she had snared the hearts of the people.

The loss of her golden goose now was troubling. She would have to move more carefully for a while, but she could just as easily use the event as a rallying point. She had no reservations against turning her people's anger and resentment toward her former colony. It was a soldier from Ymir who had abducted their idol, after all, and Ymir fighters had engaged a squadron of hers during their pursuit. She could spin it easily to them that those ships had been sent to prevent her from returning their savior to them, that she would be safely back on Eden if not for Ymir's meddling.

They would buy it easily. She could use that in turn to put pressure on Ymir to make concessions. The threat of having their food supply cut off would go a long way toward ensuring the cooperation of the council, especially now that her father... she felt a pang of something: sorrow? anger? guilt? frustration? She pushed it aside. She couldn't dwell on such things right now. Anyway, he had provided a strong personality, a rallying point to focus the other council members. Without him, they were divided and directionless.

There was one other matter to consider: what to do about Sophia and him. More mixed feelings threatened to bubble up, but she forced them down again. Whatever she decided would have to wait for some time. Her forces had made it through the furious battle, but substantial repairs were needed, and the pilots desperately needed some time to rest. It would be a few days before she could mount any kind of operation. She set the issue aside for the time being. It had been a long day, and she was exhausted. Even so, it was several hours before she was finally able to fall asleep.

# # #

Alex lay awake on the bed. He had taken the same room he had stayed in on the trip to Eden without even thinking about it. He had bid Sophie good night and now lay in the dark, unable to sleep. He wondered again if he had made the right choice. He still couldn't bear the thought of Sophie as she had been, there in the Eden temple, but was this truly any better? They were stuck alone here on a hostile world. Was dying here really better than enslavement up there? For him it was, but he had made that choice for her.

Victoria's face came unbidden to his mind, he shook his head to clear it away. He felt a twinge of guilt over the way he had acted in the temple, but it had been necessary. He had tried to snap her out of whatever had driven her to the actions she had taken. In the end, he had been forced to accept that this was in fact the real Victoria. The friend he had thought he knew so well had just been a front, and that was painful to him. He wondered now if George and all the others would see him in the same light, a fake pretending to be something he wasn't.

He tried to force such thoughts away, but they refused to relent. He had acted so decisively on Eden, but he was anything but. He wanted desperately to talk with someone, to not be alone right now, but he did not want to disturb Sophie right now. Conflicted, he tried to will himself to sleep. It was not very effective, and it was nearly dawn before he finally drifted into blissful unconsciousness.

# # #

George lay on his bunk, trying desperately to deny the revelations he had been given. Alex, his closest friend was now an enemy he had been ordered to kill. They told him it was for the safety of everyone here, that his friend was extremely dangerous. It didn't make sense. Alex a psychic? George couldn't believe it. He had known Alex all his life and he'd never seen anything unusual in all that time.

That news alone was hard to swallow and was bad enough, but on top of that had been the report of a coup on Eden, and that Victoria Barrett of all people was now in control. Was this someone's idea of a sick joke? How in the firepits of Adar could that happen? He'd heard the full report on the situation and it still sounded too ludicrous to believe. He'd known Victoria a long time as well, and though he would easily have believed she was *capable* of something like this, he had never thought she would actually attempt a coup.

As if that alone wasn't enough, Paul's death in the recent battle felt like a gaping wound to all of them. George hadn't known him as well as Liz and Claire, but he had still been a friend. Now he was gone. He could hardly think about it.

It was like some kind of bizarre dream world where everything was ludicrously mixed up. This was too much to swallow all in one day. George lay quietly in the dark room, it felt all the more empty without Alex there now. It was an absence he had felt the whole time his friend had been gone, but it was worse now. George was exhausted from the battle which had concluded a scant few hours ago, but he still tossed and turned several times before drifting off.

# # #

Sophia sat quietly on the edge of her bed. It had been a truly overwhelming day. In all honesty she had been caught completely off guard by Alex storming into the temple to rescue her. After he had been arrested, she had given up hope of ever seeing him again. She had not complained at all when Victoria had instructed her to wear the helmet again, nor had she resisted the medication. She had felt she deserved them after what had happened that day.

Even thinking of the high priest's death was painful. Guilt wracked her over her role in it. Alex had insisted it wasn't her fault, but she couldn't accept that completely. There had been other deaths afterward as well. Under the effects of the helmet and drugs, she had unflinchingly carried out Victoria's orders. Then, trapped beneath that familiar haze she had been under most of her life, he had come for her.

She'd had no idea how strong he truly was. In all her years at the center, she had never seen anything like that. She had watched with her other eyes as the struggle played out. He had glowed such a brilliant blinding green that she had been forced to look away. It was almost scary to think about now.

Even after everything she had done, he had come for her. Emotion threatened to overwhelm her. Free of the helmet, and with the effects of the drugs waning, she could feel again. She didn't know what to do with the storm raging inside her, tears, another sensation that was still new to her, streamed down her face. She lay back on the bed, swept up in the maelstrom of unfamiliar sensations before sleep mercifully claimed her.

Chapter 16

After a fitful few hours of sleep, Alex wearily sat up in bed. There wasn't much point in trying to fall asleep again. It was already late morning. He got to his feet and went about his morning ritual mechanically. After he finished, he stumbled out of the room, heading to the ship's kitchen to find some breakfast. Sophie was already seated at the table when he entered, working on a pastry. There was a moment of awkward silence as they both froze and attempted not to look at each other. Alex pushed himself to move, and stepped past to the food stores, occupying himself with browsing the considerable stock.

Finally, and with some reluctance, he selected a meal and placed it in the machine to prep it. Carefully, he took a seat at the table with Sophie. After another minute of stifling silence, he managed, "How are you feeling? Are you alright after... everything?"

She kept her eyes on her meal as she replied softly, "Yes, I'm fine. I feel a lot better this morning." She slowly lifted her head and met his eyes, there was concern in her face. "What about you? Doing all of that... it must have taken a lot out of you. I get tired quickly attempting things much less impressive than that." She couldn't talk about it in anything but those vague terms.

"I'm ok," he reassured her with a slightly tired smile. "You're right, it was pretty draining, but I'm fine now." The machine let out a beep to inform him that his meal was ready. He retrieved the package and sat again. They ate in silence for a while. He had expected himself to be famished, but after a few bites, he found himself simply shifting things around on the plate with his fork.

Sophie suddenly spoke up, startling him a bit. "Why?" she asked him in a pained voice, "Why did you come back for me?" She met his eyes now, conflicting emotion playing across her face. The question caught him off guard and it took him a moment before he was able to respond.

"What kind of question is that?" he asked her. "Of course I came back for you, I couldn't possibly leave you like that." He hesitated a moment, but pushed on anyway. "You're too important to me to even think of leaving you."

She broke down completely at that, tears flowed freely. "I don't deserve to be here," she sobbed, "I killed them, Alex. Even with all the drugs and everything, *I* was the one who did it. *Me.*"

He moved over to her, and wrapped his arms around her. She didn't pull away. She simply sat there still sobbing heavily. He sat there a moment before speaking. "Sophie," he said, softly now, "I came for you because I want you here, with me. If you were up there now, she would have kept using you to kill even more people, probably for the rest of your life." She shivered in his arms at the thought of it.

"You're free of that now." he assured her. "I'll do everything in my power to ensure you never have to go through that again." He meant every word of it. Gently, he reached out to take her chin and tilt her head up toward his. She offered no resistance as he brought his face to hers. Her eyes drew closed as their lips met. It felt right.

# # #

The air was heavy with loss as George sat watching the funeral ceremony proceed. There had been so many casualties the day before. With a full squadron halfway to Eden when the attack hit, the remaining defenders were sorely outnumbered for most of the fight. When George and the rest of the squad finally made it back, they were already bloodied from their previous fight.

Claire and Liz sat alongside him. Liz was weeping openly. She had admitted to him and Claire what they had always suspected. She and Paul had been very close, but they had been seeing each other for just six months before he was killed yesterday. Many of their former classmates were grieving close friends as well. The last time they had been in this position, Councilman Barrett had been able to help console and fortify them.

In the wake of his own tragic passing, he was sorely missed. There was no one capable of taking his place and bolstering their severely flagging morale. George couldn't remember things ever looking as dire as they did right now. The funeral ceremony continued around him, but he was oblivious to it now, caught up in his own thoughts and reminiscence.

# # #

Victoria stood at the podium erected for her in the pavilion before the temple. It was set well away from the edge—she would not make her predecessor's mistake. This was the first time she would address the masses since coming to power, and without Sophia to wow the crowd for her. She knew what needed to be done. They needed a target for the anxiety and stress that had been building since the high priest's tragic accident, and she intended to give them one.

"Citizens of the great paradise of Eden," she opened with. Massive screens projected her image for the crowd below to see clearly. "You have been sorely tested in the past few weeks. Much tragedy has befallen us, but we will not succumb to it. We are strong, and our steadfast devotion to the departed ones shall be rewarded." She paused as the cheers of approval broke out across the gathered crowds.

"There is one other matter I must speak on," she continued, "though it brings me pain even to think of it. It is my grave duty to inform you that the death of our dear high priest Isaiah was not an accident." A deafening roar of disbelief and outrage went out from the crowd. They were hungry for blood now, and she intended to deliver.

She turned to a pair of guards stationed on her left and nodded. They moved toward her bearing Commander Andrews of the Ymir Special Forces between them. She resisted the temptation to allow a smile of satisfaction to play across her face at the scowl on the man's face aimed impotently at her. As he drew close he spoke, "So you're going to use me as a scapegoat to cover for you? You really are despicable." She ignored him. His opinion no longer held any weight.

"Behold," she cried theatrically for the crowd. "This man is an operative of the Ymir special forces. His team is responsible for the assassination of our high priest, and the kidnapping of our savior, the gifted Sophia. Their treachery demands justice!"

"What are you going to do?" he sneered at her, "Shoot me?" She turned to regard him while she waited for the roars of approval from the crowd to die down.

"A simple execution will do for your team, but not you," she replied. "What I need here is an example, a rallying point. The people are crying out for justice, I intend to let them take it themselves." The formerly arrogant commander paled as her statement sunk in. She nodded again to the guards and they pulled their prisoner forward again.

This time he visibly struggled against them, but he could not free himself. The crowd surged eagerly against the barricades as they led him inexorably down the great stone steps to the waiting masses below. He managed to throw one last hate filled glare up to her before he was pushed into the teeming masses. Then he was gone.

# # #

Alex led the way as he and Sophie made their way down toward the excavation site. He held her hand firmly in his. All the awkwardness that had plagued them since their escape was gone now. They were bound together more closely than perhaps any couple had ever been. The mental bond they shared had become all the stronger now. There was hardly a need for speech. He loved her, and she loved him. Almost from the very start they had shared a connection, but now they could define it clearly.

The way was difficult. The years had not been kind to the dig site, and it was slow going. Several times, they had been forced to dig through collapsed tunnels or search for alternate routes. Eventually, they were able to make their way to the center of the excavation.

Unlike the man-made tunnels, the gigantic artifact, whatever it was, seemed completely unaffected by the passage of years. It had a metallic sheen to it, but the surface was impossibly smooth. Its vast surface curved slightly from top to bottom, distorting their reflections. Alex stepped closer, feeling almost drawn to it. Hesitantly, he reached out his hand, pausing for a moment before finally tentatively laying it on the artifact's surface.

It was slightly cool to the touch, and smooth almost to the point of slipperiness. How long had this object been here on this world? Was it natural or had it been left by some other species long vanished? Alex was so caught up in speculation that he didn't realize what was happening until he heard Sophie gasp behind him.

The surface of the object was rippling around his hand, and the once silvery surface was now pulsing in a rainbow of colors. Alarmed, he jumped back keeping Sophie behind him as he watched the object warily. The artifact began to twist and change before them. A large depression was forming in its side. The depression deepened, its sides becoming more uniform, until they formed a neat entrance with a corridor leading deeper inside. Finally, the colors faded and the object stilled, retaining its new configuration.

Alex and Sophie exchanged glances. He was curious and eager to explore this new mystery. She was reluctant, concerned for his safety. He squeezed her hand reassuringly and coaxed her into following, still reluctantly, as he stepped into the newly formed passageway. They continued forward for several minutes before they abruptly stepped into a vast chamber filled with countless devices of unknown origin. The unmistakable hum of machinery answered decisively that this artifact was indeed designed by someone for some unknown purpose.

Alex couldn't help staring at the incomprehensibly advanced machines before them. The room around them was so large that he could not make out the far side of it. Alien equipment filled almost all of that incomprehensively huge space. Of everything before them, one device stood out from the others. A raised path on the floor stretched forward a short way to what looked almost like a human terminal interface. There was no screen present, and the device in place of the keyboard was smooth and featureless, but otherwise the resemblance was striking.

He felt drawn to it, moving slowly down the walkway toward it, almost like he was in a trance. He was stopped by Sophie, still holding on to his hand, standing unmoving behind him.

"Be careful," she cautioned him. Concern was etched into her face. After all they had been through she didn't want to lose him now. He felt the same for her.

"Don't worry," he reassured her with a slight smile. "I will." The promise did little to allay her fears, but after a moment she reluctantly released his hand. He stepped up to the device, and after one more moment of hesitation, placed his hand on the keyboard-like panel. A few moments passed and nothing happened. He turned to look back at Sophie, and the world fell away around him.

# # #

"What did you say?" Victoria had heard the general's report, but automatically asked him to repeat his report to buy herself time to think. He repeated his message. There was another fleet inbound on their position, several times the size of the one they had faced the day before. Back-to-back assaults like this were unprecedented. It did not bode well for them. Their pilots were still weary and repairs had not yet been completed on some of the ships.

There was no choice. "We're up against the wall here, general." she admitted. "Hit them with everything we've got. We're not going down without a fight." She would do everything in her power to protect her world so recently acquired. She had not put forth all that effort just to have it burn around her. The general acknowledged and signed off.

Swiftly, she left her chambers and headed out across the colony toward the military ward and its command center. She wanted to be able to watch events play out and assist in any way she could. For once she cursed the scenic, rustic nature of Eden. A car would have gotten her there by now. She picked up her pace. Every second counted.

# # #

George hurried to where his fighter was being prepped for launch. The wing still bore an ugly black wound from a close shot. There hadn't been time to effect repairs. Some ships were in even worse condition. The same could be said for the pilots, still reeling from the previous fight. Liz had broken down completely and they were forced to pull her from the roster, her relatively undamaged ship assigned to someone else.

He knew he had no choice. He had to fly or everyone he knew and cared for would die at the hands of merciless machines. The thought galvanized him, giving him the strength to vault into his cockpit and begin prepping the ship for launch. It was going to be another long day.

# # #

Sensation rushed over Alex like a tidal wave, and it took every ounce of strength not to be overwhelmed and driven mad by it. He saw sounds, tasted colors, and heard smells. Experiences far beyond the comprehension of a human mind washed past him. He tried to scream, but he could make no sound. At that moment, just as he neared his breaking point, everything suddenly stopped. He was left in complete silence, and stillness. After taking a few minutes to recover, he realized he was now in a vast, empty room. The seemingly infinite space was bathed in a uniform white light. Thoughts and images came unbidden to his mind. It was communication beyond anything he had ever experienced, more direct than even the bond he shared with Sophie. Whatever was speaking to him, was doing so on a level below even the formation of organized thought; directly; mind-to-mind.

The conversation slowly stabilized to become intelligible to Alex. "Who are you?" he called out to the presence now linked to him. "What is this place?" The presence paused for some time. Subconsciously, Alex knew that it was framing its answer in a way that it thought would make sense to the small life form before it. It did not explain this; Alex just knew it to be so. Finally, it presented an explanation beyond belief.

The machine he had touched was indeed a computer terminal, but the system it was a part of was immeasurably vast. This planet and all of its moons were a part of that system; everything about them was monitored and regulated by this one computer. It had been left here long ago by another race of beings, and had run idle for ages. The computer had detected their approach and prepared the system for their arrival. Once they had landed, it began preparing to interface with them. Subtle alterations were made to unborn children during development to enable them to interface with the system. Alex, Sophie, and the other gifted were the result. This method was slow, however, and in its eagerness to interface with them, the machine had jumped when another opportunity had presented itself. The colonists artificially-intelligent robots. The excavation on the artifact had presented a way for the machine to interface with them.The computer seemed almost apologetic as it continued its explanation. It had attempted to make contact with the mechanical beings accompanying the colonists, but the unforseen result was that the robots were driven mad. Direct contact by a being far greater than they had overwhelmed their primitive minds. The computer had been forced to fall back to its original plan, but the development of the research center, and their inhibition of their abilities had interfered with that, until now.

"Why were you attempting to contact us?" Alex queried the machine. It explained that it was limited in the actions it could take. It felt a sense of responsibility for the suffering they had endured, but it was unable to resolve the situation alone. It did however, have the ability to grant *them* the ability to act as administrators and direct it into action.

The room shifted, the vast empty whiteness replaced with the black of space, stars glinting like diamonds in the expanse. The planet and its moons floated before Alex. Tiny grey specks swarmed among them, illuminated by angry flashes. A battle was taking place even now. Then, the computer zoomed the view to the area around Pavonis Prime. More ships were rising from the surface, a fleet far larger than any Alex had seen. This was it. The AI had seen the colonists' weakness and were moving in for the kill.

The computer urged him to action. He could end this conflict now. Alex hesitated. It was withholding something from him, and he could sense it. Reluctantly, it finally conveyed to him that the enormity of the task was such that he would likely not survive. Directing a system of this scale and complexity was far beyond his limits. He asked the machine for a few moments to consider, and one last chance to speak with Sophie should he accept. The machine granted his request with an urge for haste. The world fell away from him again.

\# \# \#

Victoria kept her face frozen in a mask of calm. Things looked grim indeed. They had managed to withstand the assault admirably thus far, but their entire force was committed, and enemy reinforcements continued to arrive in a steady stream. It was only a matter of time before her own forces were overwhelmed. All around her, top brass barked orders and studied displays showing the battle above them.

Some had approached her about evacuating the city, or moving the populace to shelters, but she had vetoed the suggestion; there was no point to it. They had nowhere to run to. The other colonies were facing the same scale of attacks as Eden was, and she didn't have anywhere near the capacity to transport everyone anyway. Evacuations would only cause a panic. The only choice they had now was to fight like hell and hope that somehow it might be enough.

\# \# \#

They couldn't keep this up. George had to accept it. There was no way they could hold off the enemy at this rate. New ships joined the battle to replace each kill the humans managed. Every able pilot and flight-worthy fighter were already committed. More than anything, he wished his friends could be up here with him now. Alex, Paul, and even Victoria. He felt their absence even more keenly here in this desperate bid for the survival of their world.

He set his sights on a pair of fighters, and let out a salvo of laser fire. His shots connected with the rearmost craft and clipped one of its wings clean off. It veered away, unable to maintain course. His second shot bubbled armor off the rear of the other fighter. It dove sharply, trying to shake him. He matched the maneuver and drilled a bolt right through it, destroying the craft. *That's two down,* he told himself, *and about a hundred more to go.*

# # #

Alex blinked... He was back in reality. The vast hall of machines surrounded him once more. He turned to see Sophie still standing with a look of concern on her face. She asked in confusion, "What? Nothing happened?" Alex didn't understand what she was saying.

"What do you mean?" he asked, "what did you see?"

"You walked up and touched that thing just a few seconds ago, and nothing happened, what are you asking me for?"

He explained as best he could what he had experienced to her. It was difficult to put into words. When he finished, she simply stared at him incredulously. "Are you sure you're feeling ok?" she asked him, worry evident in her face. She must think he was crazy.

He took her hands in his and met her eyes. "Trust me," he implored her. "It was all real. Right now everyone out there in the colonies is fighting desperately for survival. I have a chance to fix all of this right here, right now. This is something only I can do." His eyes pleaded for her to understand.

"You have to come back to me." Her eyes would brook no argument. "Promise me that," she pleaded. He drew her close and wrapped his arms around her.

"I promise," he told her. In truth, he had no idea if he would be able to fulfill the promise, but he resolved to do everything in his power to try. They stood like that a while before he reluctantly broke off the embrace. She stepped back, making no attempt to prevent him from doing what he had to. He stepped purposefully toward the strange device once more, and placed his hand on the smooth panel. Once again, the world fell away around him.

# # #

The calm, purposeful order that had once ruled the command center had transitioned into near panic. The situation was beyond grim. There were now too few *Seraphs* remaining to hold off the invading fleet. Several ships were already within the atmosphere. Victoria slammed her fist into the console in front of her, bringing temporary silence to the chamber.

"I want every able body capable of carrying a weapon, armed and deployed to repel ground forces," she ordered, forcing a calm commanding tone. The officers present understood the futility of the order, but hastened to obey regardless. She had resolved before that if this was to be her end, she would go down fighting. They would pay for every inch of ground they took. She swore it.

# # #

It was over. They had failed. George was exhausted and battered, watching more and more enemy ships slip past the beleaguered defensive screen. It was impossible to stop them all, there were too many of them, and only a handful of *Valkyries* remained. This was his worst nightmares made manifest. Again and again, he pushed himself to take down a ship just to have three more push past unchallenged. He pushed harder, determined to make their defeat as costly as he could.

# # #

Once again, Alex found himself floating in the void. The familiar Delta Pavonis system floated around him. The situation had visibly worsened in his absence. AI ships were landing on all three moons now and it was only a matter of time before those moons fell. The computer expressed its appreciation at his decision to return, tinged with what almost felt like relief.

Now it fell to him to protect the tiny enclaves of humanity, desperately clinging to life here in a hostile system far from their world of origin. The task would demand every ounce of strength he had, and more. He was ready. He had no regrets. He focused his entire being on the task ahead of him.

The computer presence, bound to him in this effort, surged to life. Ancient circuitry, some of which had lain dormant for centuries, hummed with renewed life. Everywhere across the system, Alex's will was transmitted and carried out.

# # #

Victoria stood alongside what security officers remained, surrounded by the ordinary citizens of Eden. Each wielded whatever weapon they could find, ready to give their lives to defend their home and loved ones. There were too few guns to go around, and some were left to carry crude farming implements or industrial tools to face the approaching robot army. They were managing to slow the advancing tide of machines, but they could not stop them. Again and again the humans were forced to give ground. Each stand they made cost the lives of more colonists, and now they had been pushed back nearly to the walls of the city itself.

Then, a miracle happened. That was the only way Victoria could describe what took place before her very eyes. The machines writhed and convulsed as if struggling against an unseen force. Some were tossed about like rag dolls, others were squeezed and compacted into useless scrap. She had seen this before! Victoria whirled around and scanned the crowd of desperate defenders around her, but he wasn't here. Of course he wasn't. Then how was this happening?

The colonists around her, stunned into inaction at first, now cheered and rallied. They pressed forward to dispatch the few remaining enemies left standing. It was simple for these colonists to explain: the gods they worshipped had delivered them in their hour of need, and while Victoria would certainly use that belief to her advantage, she herself knew differently. With the situation on the ground under control, she sprinted back to the command center to check on the battle raging above them.

# # #

George could scarcely believe what he was seeing. He must have lost it. That was the only explanation. The enemy ships before him were falling by the drove, but not due to the efforts of the defenders. Some simply crumpled, as if they had been squeezed by enormous pressure. Some collided with each other, detonating brilliantly. The interceptors flying among the larger drop ships flitted erratically, unable to comprehend what was attacking their wards.

A cheer went up over the com, the remaining defenders rallied and plunged back into the fray. None of them understood what was happening, but now they had a chance and they were eager to take it. For some reason, Alex's face rose unbidden in George's mind. He shook the image away, completely focused on the fight.

# # #

All throughout the system, the purge continued. Alex was operating far beyond his limits. He had resolved to purge not only the fleets assaulting the three moons, but also every last AI unit on the planet itself. One way or another, he would end this threat today. The computer warned him again of the incredible strain he was placing on himself, but he ignored it. He would see this through to the end.

With the forces of this vast network focused against them, the robots were utterly unable to comprehend what was happening to them. Most did not even attempt to resist the god-like powers that had come to claim them. This was far beyond the scope of their comprehension, much like the brush of contact that had driven them mad to begin with. He almost felt some small measure of pity for them as they were torn apart by forces beyond their awareness.

The strain was beginning to overwhelm him as he neared the end of his task. There were only a few more matters to resolve and he pressed forward with them. The edges of his vision began to go black as he forced himself to finish. There! He had done it, but he was utterly spent.

"*Alex!*" A voice, filled with panic was calling out to his mind. Disoriented, he was unable to place it at first. "*Alex!*" it called again in desperation. Sophie, he knew it now. At that, he slowly pushed forward to full consciousness. His eyes slowly opened, her tear-streaked face, etched with fear was close to his. He managed a weak smile and she sobbed with relief, wrapping her arms around him where he lay on the floor of the machine chamber.

He didn't remember crossing back into reality, it must have happened while he was unconscious. With effort, he managed to push himself to a sitting position. She clung to him all the while. "I promised you didn't I?" He reassured her gently, wrapping an arm around her.

"Don't ever scare me like that again!" she chastised him, still clinging tightly. A moment later she asked, "Did it work?" She looked up into his face worriedly.

"Yes," he told her. "It's done. The bots are gone—for good." He pushed himself to stand, he was shaky and weak, and he was forced to lean on her to manage.

"Don't push yourself," she urged him, "Just rest a moment." Concern was still visible on her face.

"Don't worry," he replied, "I'm alright. There's something I want to show you." Carefully, they made their way out of the room and back down the strange tunnel back to the excavation site. Once they stepped out, he laid his hand on the strange surface again. It rippled once more, and the hall slowly reverted away to the impossibly smooth wall, just as before. There was no trace of the passage or the room behind it.

# # #

With some effort, Sophie helped Alex climb back through the tunnels to emerge onto the surface of the planet once more. The sun was now high in the sky. Several hours had passed while they were below. They were also no longer alone! Sophie stared in disbelief at the cluster of people gathered around their shuttle. They were looking around in confusion, trying to understand where they were, and how they had suddenly gotten there.

Sophie realized that she recognized them! Many times in the dead of night, she had reached out to them for comfort, and they had reached out to her. They were all here, every last gifted individual who had been confined in the research center. She turned to Alex in shock and surprise, but he merely smiled. They made their way over to the confused group, to greet them warmly and welcome them to their new home.

# # #

Victoria stood in the command center, receiving reports and directing efforts for clean up, and treatment for those who had been wounded in both the battle above and on the ground. They were in bad shape all around, but they were alive. Right now, that was all that mattered. All of the attackers had been destroyed, down to the last. Her generals could offer no explanation for what had happened, nor could her scientists. She knew what they did not, but she could not answer how he had managed it.

Reports had come in from Ymir and Adar. They had experienced the same miracles that had occurred here. The implications of that were not comforting, nor was the report that all of the gifted at the Ymir research center had suddenly and inexplicably vanished. That lent credence to what she had suspected, but it was still troubling. She could not focus on that now however, her people needed her, and she would not let them down.

# # #

George sat unmoving in the cockpit of his stationary fighter, surveying the scene around him. Nearby space was littered with the remains of dozens of ships which mere minutes before had been bearing down on the only home he had ever known. His mind made no attempt to rationalize what he had just seen. It was beyond any possible explanation he could grasp.

The all clear came in over the com, and he mechanically went through the motions of bringing the ship around and plotting in a return course. The losses had been horrendous, but they would survive. They had been given a chance, and he was determined to make the most of it.

Chapter 17

Victoria stood once more before the podium in the temple pavilion. It fell upon her to provide closure to her people after the events only a week ago when they had desperately struggled for their very survival. She recalled a time not so long ago when her father had done the same back on Ymir just before she had set out on her journey.

She recognized that at the time, she would have been unable to measure up to him that day, but she had grown a great deal since then. Her brief reign here had taught her much through the hardships she had faced. She chose to believe that if he were here to see her now, he would indeed give her the approval she had so desperately craved.

The earpiece she wore signaled an incoming call, and she activated it, there were still a few moments before the ceremony would begin. "Yes?" she spoke into the mouthpiece.

"We've reached the landing site and examined the area as you requested," the operative reported. As soon as she had been able, she had sent a team to the planet to investigate the point where Alex had set down, convinced there was some clue there to recent events.

"The shuttle itself is here, but there is no sign of any people anywhere in the vicinity. The site seems to be some kind of mining site; there are several buildings present with intact terminals. We're doing a dump of the data now." So they had moved on. Very well, she had no reason to pursue them now. She felt only the slightest twinge of regret as she let go any hope of seeing him again.

He had made his choice as she had made hers. "Very well," she informed the agent, "Keep me informed of anything you learn about the site. Don't bother searching for the passengers, they're likely long gone by now." The operative acknowledged and disconnected.

She turned her thoughts away from what might have been and concentrated on the present. Her people needed her now as much as ever. There was a great deal of repairing and healing to be done in the wake of the nightmares they had faced. She vowed she would guide them through this, and any storms the future may hold.

Epilogue

Alex sank his toes into the lush grass beneath him, caught up in the brilliant blue of the open sky. It had been one month since he and Sophie had first landed on the surface of this vacant world. Sophie now stood at his side, her hand in his. They were on the outskirts of a small rural town they had discovered a short distance from the mining site where they had first landed.

All of the buildings here were in perfect condition. Either they had been abandoned before the war reached this area, or they had been inexplicably repaired as the mining camp had been. The small town was ideal for their needs. There was space and shelter here for everyone Alex had liberated from the research center.

Additionally, the abandoned crops and livestock tended by the town's former inhabitants had managed to thrive, even in their absence. There was more than enough food to go around. Alex and several of the others had eagerly dived into the task of bringing the fields and herds to order.

Working with his hands to create rather than destroy brought a great sense of accomplishment to him. They had slowly but steadily built the beginning of a primitive but happy lifestyle here. He had no complaints, no longing for any of the luxuries he had left behind. Here they could be at peace.

He turned his head to look at Sophie. She was so beautiful standing there next to him. There was a glow to her that had not been there when he had first met her not so long ago. She noticed him looking at her, and turned to smile up at him. There was no awkwardness between them now; they both knew exactly how the other felt.

One of the younger children came running up to them to tell them that lunch was ready. They followed as he eagerly pulled them along toward the main building. The change in all of the former test subjects had been as dramatic as it had been with Sophie. They had worked patiently with each of them to help them adjust to their new way of life. Now there was nothing to distinguish them from any other person. Alex had not used any of his abilities since that day, except for some occasional telepathy. Neither had any of the others to his knowledge, though there had been no official decision regarding the matter. They simply desired to live a normal life here. They had left their abilities behind with the other remnants of their past lives.

Alex, Sophie, and the little boy reached the door to the main building, probably once a town hall. Several of the children seated at the table called out a greeting to them as they came into view. Alex smiled as he stepped into the room. It was good to be home.

# # #

Lieutenant George Simmons walked slowly down the line of new cadets. He inspected each as he passed, evaluating the nervous, potential pilots as they stood at attention. Had he looked like this when he had stood in their place a year before? Had it truly only been a year since then? It seemed like ages had passed.

In the wake of the devastating losses one month ago, many young pilots had found themselves promoted to fill voids left by officers killed in combat. George still did not feel qualified for the rank, but he performed to the best of his abilities to be worthy of the honor.

He reached the end of the row and turned to Commander Prescott who was currently in charge of the batch. The aged professor had recovered somewhat from the loss of his son last month, but the fire was still gone from his eyes, perhaps forever.

Prescott smiled warmly as he greeted George, which surprised him somewhat. He had only known the man as a superior, and it was awkward to be on near equal terms now. He took the man's proffered hand and shook it firmly.

"A sorry lot you've got here professor," he informed Prescott. "They need to be whipped into shape." A hint of a spark flickered in the old man's eye at that, and he gave George a calculating smile.

"Indeed," he replied, "I haven't seen such a disappointing batch of cadets in all my years here at the academy. They practically reek of mediocrity." He turned toward the cadets with a scowl. "Alright you sorry lot, head to the simulators and try not to completely shame your families with your performance." The cadets filed out as quickly as they could manage, and George managed to stifle his laughter with some effort.

Once the cadets were out of earshot he asked Prescott, "Were we really like that when we started out?"

The old soldier grinned back at him, "Oh, most definitely. Somehow I always manage to turn them around, even lost causes like you!" George gave a hearty laugh at that. Despite all the hardship they had endured, Ymir colony would survive. That was enough for him.

# # #

Victoria sat at her desk, busily working her way through mounds of paperwork that had piled up. Running a world was not as glamorous as she had expected, but she had no intention of running from a challenge. The rewards justified the effort she had expended, and she was content with her place in life.

Eden had suffered in the last battle as much as the other colonies, but over the past month they had made great progress in working back to full strength. The complete cessation of attacks from the planet had enabled them to apply the substantial resources they had reserved for defense toward rebuilding instead.

If anything, that terrible day had cemented her role here beyond her wildest expectations. Her presence on the front lines, risking her own life to defend her people had endeared her to the colonists of Eden more so than any speech she could have made.

The dramatic and mysterious destruction of their oppressors had also reaffirmed to the people that their gods were indeed watching over them. The city was practically exploding with zeal in the wake of the attacks. Shockingly, she had even heard reports that colonists on Ymir and Adar were seeking to make pilgrimages here, convinced that they had been saved by supernatural forces.

Her thoughts turned invariably toward the planet below, as they always did when she recalled that day. She wondered again, what he was doing. She truly did have feelings for him back when she began that fantastic journey. Time had lessened the blow of his rejection, and she could think about him now with few feelings of regret.

Now, she honestly wished him and Sophia well, wherever they were. They deserved some peace after all they had done for their fellow man. She had no lingering concern for the dire warnings issued by Commander Andrews. Even if Alex was a threat to them, he had very clearly demonstrated that he was beyond their ability to control or stop.

She turned her attention back to her work, allowing herself only a small sigh. No time to dwell on the past. She needed to focus on the future. Her people, for they truly were her people now, were relying her. In the beginning, she had merely desired the power and prestige of this position and to escape from her father's shadow, but she felt she had grown into the role. She truly cared for them now.

She focused on the documents before her, caught up in her work. Her ambition had been sated. Together, she and her two onetime companions truly had changed the world.

About the Author

Joshua McCullough was born in Landstuhl, Germany. Raised in a military family, he has lived all across the United States. He has been a QA tester for Microsoft Game Studios, and is now a crewmember at Nonpareil Institute, where he works in game design. *The Secret of Delta Pavonis* is his first novel.

About the Publisher

Nonpareil Institute is a 501(c)3 nonprofit corporation dedicated to enhancing the lives of people with Autism. We train and employ adults and young adults on the Autism Spectrum in technology and the arts. Some students become programmers or game designers, while others become authors, artists, or musicians. Our dream is to build a worldwide chain of self-sustaining campuses where these people can work and live in an environment that understands and nurtures them.